The
Shaver Mystery Magazine
Vol II No 3 1948

Richard S. Shaver
Alfred Steber (Editor)

SAUCERIAN PUBLISHER
Original Sources in Ufology

ISBN: 978-1-955087-55-1

9 781955 087551

2023, Saucerian Publisher

PROLOGUE

Returning to the classics in any genre is generally a good idea. This also goes for UFO literature. Rereading a book or reviewing old documents after ten or twenty years is a rewarding experience. You will discover new data and ideas you didn't notice before. The reason, of course, is that you are, in many ways, not the same person reading the book the second or third time. Hopefully, you have advanced in knowledge, experience, and intellectual and spiritual discernment. A good starting point is to reread the UFO classics to understand the more profound mystery of what happened during that era.

This title is scarce and hard to find these days. The Shaver Mystery Magazine originally was published by the Shaver Mystery Club. This newsletter published the first printed stories on UFOs and was a major forum for debates about the occult, Forteans, and Lemurians. As Ray Palmer promoted it: "dedicated to the further study of the hidden truths as presented in the fact-fiction stories by Richard S. Shaver..."

In essence, the Shaver Mystery is a collection of stories in which Shaver claimed to have discovered proof of an evil humanity in underground caverns. Shaver portrayed an alien race that resided in Earth's caverns before escaping, leaving behind two distinct populations of offspring: the "Teros," a benevolent group of humanoids, and the "Deros," or "detrimental robots," a vile race who tormented and devoured humans. The Deros were especially brutal to women. The tales encouraged the establishment of Shaver Mystery Clubs.

The present edition is an authentic reproduction of the original Shaver Mystery Magazine printed text in shades of gray. **IMPORTANT,even though we have attempted to maintain the integrity of the original work, the present facsimile reproduction may have missing letters and blurred pages, poor pictures due to the age of the original scanned copy.** This magazine has been formatted from its original version for publication. Great, but unpretentious, this issue is an extraordinarily rare symbol of what was going on in those early years of the modern UFO phenomena.

Editor
Saucerian Publisher, 2023

The SHAVER MYSTERY MAGAZINE

Being dedicated to the further study of the hidden truths as presented in the fact-fiction stories by Richard S. Shaver, made famous in the past three years in AMAZING STORIES magazine.

Subscription Price 50c per Issue

OBTAINED ONLY

THROUGH MEMBERSHIP

THE SHAVER MYSTERY CLUB

CONTENTS

| VOL. II | 1948 | NO. 3 |

EDITORIAL . . . . Page 4

READER'S SECTION
By The Readers . . . . Page 5

MANDARK
By Richard Shaver . . . . Page 6

Interior Illustration by Virgil Finlay

ARTICLE - "Concerning Mr. Palmer's Letters and
Mr. Shaver's Inertia"
By Robert Kidwell . . . . Page 22

REPLY TO ROBERT KIDWELL
By Richard S. Shaver . . . . Page 27

Frontispiece by Virgil Finlay

THE SHAVER MYSTERY MAGAZINE

is Published by

RICHARD S. SHAVER, EDITOR & PUBLISHER

RT. 2 BOX 74, LILY LAKE,
McHENRY, ILLINOIS

❧ EDITORIAL ❧

NOW, free of other duties, your editor will have the time to devote proper attention to this magazine. I am sorry that has not been true in the past.

We plan to tell the whole truth, except those truths that might hurt someone, even innocently. And not any lies at all.

We will try to tell you all the truth that is now hidden from you, however hard the job may be. Most truths are good.

It is true that only people who understand the Shaver Mystery know anything about life on this planet. I want to congratulate all you readers who have realized this and resubscribed to this effort to publicize the deepest secret of this planet.

The winning of knowledge takes men into dark and ugly places, and only there can men find the dwelling places of the evils that plague them. And learn what to do to combat those evils. It is only in such places that men can learn truly what is needed to make life better than it is.

We plan to tell these truths to you, just as long as the liars who hide them from you can take it and keep on lying. When that lie is dead our job is done.

A great many people in this country know the Shaver-Mystery is a true mystery, and keep quiet about it through fear.

Such fear is not a healthy thing to live with, and they have to live with it.

An augmentation ray can make such a fear a terrible and an ugly force in a man's mind. Such augmentation is used on people, unknown to themselves.

Such a man becomes a dangerous character in time.

We have such dangerous characters in our society, and we do not recognize them. We devote our attention to simpler scandals and slanders.

But we should ask such a fear ridden person what they know about the caves, or about "Forbidden Fruit" or . . . any of a number of such secret names and phrases, and watch the fear come in their face. Then you know that what you see is not a man, but a fear that lies to you.

Such men are not friends, they keep too many needed things closed from men's eyes.

A friend is someone who tells you the truth that is good for you to know. A friend is someone you can call on at any hour of the day or night for help.

A friend is the greatest value on earth. They are rare, and when we have them, we do not know, often until too late.

Some of us use our friends too much. Others do not use their friends enough, and friendship dies of lack of circulation.

Some trust their friends too much, and then condemn them when they slip and break something.

Some trust their friends too little, being always suspicious of their intent, and ready to believe slander about them.

But in the world we will have when the telaug is brought up from the caverns and manufactured and distributed for sale to everyone—we will all have lots of friends.

For we will be able to know truly what our friends think, and mistakes can't happen to destroy friendship.

We will all know then whether our wife really loves us or not, and evil intent will perish from the light of others reason watching it.

The telaug is the most needed tool of our life.

It is one of the greatest reasons for the secrecy, because of the advantage it is supposed to give the minority.

Men could build the telaug today, and the whole mass of error and suspicion would vanish, our social life become clean.

Help make that come true!

READER'S SECTION

Each issue we will publish as many pertinent letters to the Shaver Mystery as space allows. We urge all readers to contribute any facts, personal or otherwise, to help our research.

Dear Mr. Shaver:

When Mr. Shaver's now full grown mystery was in its infancy I wrote one short letter or rather note to Amazing Stories suggesting that the whole thing be quietly and completely squelched. I assume others must have written similar letters but I have yet to see any letters published in either Amazing Stories or your club magazine which might prove to have a retarding action against Shaver's hysterical claims. If, as you said in your build up for this Shaver Club the magazine is going to act as a melting pot for all evidence for and against the Shaver Myster as well as all comments and opinions for and against it, I defy you to publish this letter and let it draw its own results.

Let us begin at the beginning. Mr. Shaver claims to have been in these caves, as I recall, not once but several times. Then, surely, he must know of at least one way to re-enter the caves. With so many people (as I note from published letters in the Club Magazine) ready and willing to finance and accompany a "safari" into the caves, what is detaining Mr. Shaver from organizing and leading said "Safari"? Also, since he has made repeated visits to the caves does not Mr. Shaver have one single solitary shred of physical undeniable evidence to uphold his hallucinations?

So far Shaver's claims have been basically proofless unless one is gullible and imaginative enough to accept his word for them, I for one, am not. Mr. Shaver claims that narrow minded persons will react to his story in exactly the same fashion that I am. A good argument but a false one. I am no more narrow minded than any other human being. Until the atom bomb was exploded and I could actually see the explosions and view the aftermath I would have firmly doubted that human endeavor could have brought about such a caclysmic power. Likewise I shall genuinely doubt Mr. Shaver's yapping until I see one of his ancient rays at work. Or until I can view the results of these rays. Or for that matter, until solid material proof is laid before me so that I may examine it minutely, and personally.

I am most ready and willing to admit that extra terrestrial forces may touch upon earth occasionally and cause phenomena with which our minds cannot cope, or that these alien forces may be continuously at work here doing things we have no knowledge of. But Mr. Shaver says these space ships which visit earth in secrecy, occasionally are seen by human beings. Is there any area where they have been seen consistently? No mention has been made of one and I would like to know if there is such a place?

In regard to our space ships also, isn't it a little on the ridiculous side to have persons able to build and operate craft that cross the ether, stop at earth and pick up loads of refrigerators and washing machines? Surely a mind capable of devising such machines as space ships would not have to use those space ships to come to Earth to get a washing machine!

Now a few miscellaneous questions for my friend Mr. Shaver to answer (publicly and sensibly, if he dares) and I shall desist. What do the people of the caverns eat and where do they get it? It must take a staggering amount of food to feed the teeming life of the caverns. How are these incredibly deep caverns ventilated? Since there are miles of them underground, massive and extensive ventilation systems would be a necessity. It's a known fact that explosions in mines (other than those controlled by the operators) are caused by subterranean gasses collecting and expending in unused sections of the mines. Do none of Mr. Shavers caverns collect gasses and explode? Also, our mines are (in comparison to the caves) just barely under the surface and yet need immense heave, and complicated shoring to keep them from collapsing. Since Mr. Shaver's caverns were built to house a race of giant people and not just a handful of ordinary sized miners, how does he explain the fact that, although beyond measure in age these immense dwelling have not collapsed or had seepage of underearth water into them? (Which of course, would weaken them and cause collapse.) Where do the cave dwellers secure their clothing, medical supplies, luxuries, and all the comforts associated with living as we know it today?

And since these nasty people are all powerful, and have machines that can see the surface of the earth and that can reach up and kill by the mere turning of a switch, what keeps them from destroying a person so obviously bent on giving away the secret of their existence as is Mr. Shaver? Remember, now, that they have successfully kept this secret since before the very birth of Christ, himself, so why shouldn't our practically omniprescient cavern killers

(Continued on Page 33)

MANDARK

By RICHARD S. SHAVER

Continuing the tremendous 200,000 word Novel
- - - the true story of the Life of Christ

CHAPTER VII

NOW for long months she studied the mind of the young God, always keeping his will submerged and subservient to her will by the regulation of the rheostats controlling the flows of energy to and from the augmentation device which probed always with its rays the many facets of the mighty Elder-brain of Yahveh.

And just as hers had been to his subservient, so to her's was his mind now the complete and unwilling servant—while the machine had been in its former polarity of flow—he had been dominant—and now the whole was reversed, and herself the controlling will of the hook-up. Now her vile and selfish thought swept through his mind with such augmentation that he could not help but obey—as it were his own will, and his mighty mind became but a pitiful tool of her lust and will to dominate all life in the caverns. Yahveh now acted and thought as she desired, for no flesh can make a greater will than a dynamo can turn out synthetic will-currents of force—and Yahveh was now but an extra member of her body, always there to do her thinking when she so desired, though there was no compulsion for her to listen to his advice or wisdom and indeed he could only think of those inconsequential and lustful things with which her mind was filled.

Now was the magic of the ancient science all hers, except for the "slight" detail that she would never direct its use wisely, and this was a time of great torment to the young godling. For his mind itself was not his own, and was always at work solving the problems her evil will—for at the turn of the switch that had flooded his mind with the augmentations of her thought cells—the little thing that was the cell-ego of his mind was, as it were, no longer in the world, its voice being overwhelmed in its commands to the perceptive and cognition centers—and they heard only Lila Onderde's thought instead. There was now no Yahveh—but only Lila Onderde with the mighty brain of Yahveh at her belt —at her command, and Yahveh Jehovah would not come into existence again until that switch was turned off.

His own thought-voice was heard by Lila as a still, small, shrill voice in the great thunder of her own thought, but the God's own mind could not hear it—for it was overwhelmed and carried away by the nature of the flows and their direction within the complex mechanism.

And Lila could listen to all this thunder of augmented thoughts, or to Yahveh's thought voice alone, or to none of it—but Yahveh could never cease to be ruled by the will that was Lila's, for Lila kept always several slaves who kept the detector rays upon her mind so the great augmentive tubes were never without their supply of her will to augment—Yahveh was never without the displacement of his ego by hers which the machine was designed to bring about. And Yahveh was now not present, but Lila Onderde was present instead in his body, and she did not propose to leave. And the thought of Yahveh was never heard now even by Lila, but instead only Yahveh's thought as caused to exist by the impulses from Lila's will—which was not the same thing at all.

The God's mind and his clever fingers which had come back into use again were now always at work for her. And during this time Lila learned all the ancient wisdom and science which her mind was capable of absorbing, and for that matter she could no longer tell when it was her mind thinking or the subservient mind of Yahveh doing it for her. But because of her dominating will all his good thought and determining logic which would have made her a sane and useful person were overlooked by her in her search for ways and means of defeating all the other powers of the underworld which might threaten her.

As time went on this strange team became the paramount rulers of the underworld. The armies and rolling "Onton" cars and Lila's ray-tanks swept ever outward from the city under Jerusalem—and ever the ignorant monarchs of the other caverns gave up their

holdings to her, gave tribute and acknowledged her sovereignty, or miserably died fighting to defend their freedom.

The lovely, evil body of Lila Onderde, equipped now with the super-mind of a son of the Gods—was invincible in subtlety, in intricate treachery and swift overwhelming concentration of fighting force where no ordinary man would have looked for the single face of an enemy. And swiftly her power grew, and men of fame and wisdom and great power came to acknowledge her their Queen, and to serve and learn of her the magic of the ancient machines. But Lila was not over-generous with any information that might be used against her.

She now ruled all the caverns south of the mediterranean.

And year by year the evil power of the new and terrible Circe of the caverns grew and grew, and Lila Onderde was the "supreme one"—the talk of the cavern life everywhere on earth—and all men feared her and spoke of her beauty and its evil ways.

She now took many lovers from among the young men who served her, and Yahveh looked on, indeed it was always to him as his own body that had become a woman's, and wallowed in all manner of sin. And Yahveh was powerless to stay her will, for it was as his own.

NOW Lila had learned how the ancient beneficial ray machines were repaired and made serviceable again, and how the great projection machines were used over long distances, even through the rock and up in the surface world—to make all the surface men wonder and worship the miracles of wonder and pictured seeming life which they thought to be the work of some real and living God. But it was only Lila or some young fool of the caverns whom she allowed to use the great machines, only the demented degenerates under an evil rule, who worked such miracles now.

Much of the ancient wisdom she absorbed, though much of it was too great in scope for her mind. Her mind was too poor a vessel to contain the mighty thought—but now added was all the infinity of convolutions of Yahveh's mind added to her own—and no one could tell whether Lila was thinking—or whether Yahveh was thinking under her command—indeed neither could they tell which was which anymore.

Not wisdom or good will, she did not learn those. She did learn how to use the vast old weapons so that no other ray warriors of the ignorant cavern life could defeat her, in the same way that Yahveh had used the weapons to hold off for so long the whole raging army sent against him by her father.

Too, she learned how to appear vastly more beautiful by playing steadily over herself a flood of antique sex-stimulative rays, the "stim" of modern secret science. It delighted her evil heart to force the mind and fingers of Yahveh to operate those stim machines with all his wizardry at the complex controls used by her will to seduce the mind and arouse the love of some young man, and make of him a helpless slave for love of her—who would not otherwise have thought of looking upon her with love.

But the helpless slave-work of Yahveh upon the keys of the emotion and stim organ-devices was still the powerful God-work at which he had been trained—no man but was Lila's slave now, for Yahveh's skill made him so, at her command.

It delighted her increasingly evil heart to force the mind and fingers of Yahveh to operate these machines while she seduced ever greater and greater numbers of men to her bed—and the whoring of Lila Onderde became a legend of the caves. (The whore of Babylon, who was a similar character, mentioned in the Bible—was also a character who did her seducing with rays.)

This enslavement of Yahveh to her wishes became a large part of the satisfaction of her life, and he became the endlessly helpful but helpless to help himself—the slave of all her evil desires and habits—the pander of all her evil and continuous dissipations which, by the use of the antique magic, became a terrible whirlpool of sin and evil under Jerusalem which sucked in and destroyed all the good life of the world below and south of the mediteranean.

Lila became ever a greater and greater devil, as her terrible hereditary weakness made of her ever a more and more typical Onderde—a family known for an age as the Onderde devil-rulers. It delighted her increasingly lustful body to cause the mutilated body of Yahveh to serve her evil passions in the night with his own wrecked beauty—and the helpless soul of Yahveh revolted, but his body served the powerful dynamos of the stim-augment rays of the apparatus by which she had enslaved him. And this became a habit with her, to debauch the helpless body of Yahveh to her will. And endless were the evils and dissipations she forced upon him, trying to make him truly hers forever and the servant of evil passions.

So it was that a more terrible Circe than the caverns had ever known was come again and more greatly to the caverns, one with all the knowledge of the Elder Gods at her command in the subservient mind of Yahveh.

This evil, yet wise Lila of the terrible degenerate race of the caverns, became thus a power to be feared wherever any mind of any man had knowledge of the Elder world of caverns and all its intricate and terrible history.

When she did not know a thing, there was always waiting the broken body and helplessly laboring mind of Yahveh to serve her purpose, there was always his mind to refer to in time of need.

Thus it was that Lila became as great a power in her way as any ruler of the caverns ever was anywhere, as ever was the latter—God Pluto—as ever the latter—God Jupiter of Rome, or Zeus of Olympus, or Odin of the far north, or Osiris and Isis under Egypt, that terrible pair who ruled Egypt for so long in such absolute power.

NOW Lila's people were hereditary members of a vast religion—a cult of the underworld. That cult was the same as the one called "Satanism" in medieval times, and called "Witchcraft" and "Black Magic" and various other names. And Lila inherited with her rule over the cavern kingdom the office of High Priest of Satan, the mystic Devil-God himself.

Now in the course of the regular ceremonies of worship to Sathanas, the legendary Devil-God, Lila conceived a brilliant idea—and proceeded to carry it out. By clever hallucinations and projections, Lila made of Yahveh's tortured, twisted body—an accepted embodiment of Sathanas, the Black Rebel God himself. And the value to her of this was that she also showed quite plainly to all that this Sathanas (Yahveh) was her slave,—and his twisted and broken limbs and terrific God-like head—became under her suggestion and projection the accepted embodiment of Sathanas—and it was quite evident that this famous witch and priestess of Evil was the mistress of the immortal and held him close under her thumb. And her fame grew greatly because of this trick, and all the wide-spread cult of Sathanas worship—the same religion of which we hear in medieval times—became her tool and her subjects were more numerous than any other rulers because of this deception. And her beauty became accepted as immortal, and her power feared as an immortal's—for was not the immortal Sathanas himself her willing obedient servant, prisoner and lover?

Across the Mediteranean Rome thundered on its pompous, bloody path, and above Lila Onderde's head and miles of rock, Jerusalem the "Golden" festered on its subservient, corrupt path as a Roman satellite—but, under Jerusalem, the power of Lila Onderde grew daily by great steps, grew yearly into a vast overwhelming might which no other ruler of all the cavern world might face.

Daily she walked, naked and beautiful, before them all as the lewd avid priestess of cult's rites had been held for endless centuries—herself serving as the high priestess of this evil worship of the Dark One—the Devil himself—and Yahveh was indeed become the Devil with Lila's will animating all his helpless thinking and being.

Daily she walked, naked and beautiful, before them all as the lewd avid priesttess of sin triumphant—or ornamented with peacock's feathers and gold bangles of the exquisite antique Elder work, with pearls from the east in ropes about her neck, a girdle of hell-fire rubies about her sleek waist, the Red Mask of the Devil upraised on her hair, her face showing bright, ruby-lipped and flushed with triumphant sin beneath, her mouth avid for the sensations life was supplying her more miraculously and plentifully every day than all her youthful dreams had anticipated.

Lila was living to the full.

The black smoke rises from torches set about the great hall, in slow evil twists, and the yellow light is shed fitfully over the feasters, who are mostly rather small men, often deformed and horrible to the eye, for the strange heredity of the caverns had brought fearful changes to the forms of many—great lumpish skins, twisted limbs, and beastlike faces. The Satanists, the worst of the people of this Abyss, do not often let surface men see these deformities—instead over the ray projections, they pretend to be of God-like proportions and beauty even as they proselyte, automatically, for the Prince of Evil. Some are clad in dirt and rags, diseased, with madness glaring from their eyes —the Satanists are not always lovely to look upon. But some are clad in cloth of Gold, and their fingers gleam with jewels, their belts are set with rubies and diamonds—and all the pomp of Hell itself is wrapped about them as they worship Satan—and the lust of Lila Onderde.

These are the lowest things that earth has bred in the shape of man. They do not always have the sense to keep clean, or to think as men do—but they have a value—and it lies in a cleverness and quickness, a knowledge of the ancient mech they have grown up with, and a willingness to use the same in any vile way their master bids.

This cleverness and quickness of the hands and eyes is something they acquire very young or die.

For the mad ones of the wilder stretches or caverns, and most of the caves are wild, unexplored, even today—survival depends upon constant watchfulness and skill with a ray beam similar in some ways to the art of fencing with a rapier. No training can make up for the skill acquired by the mad ones in their constant fighting with the mech-ray weapons from their childhood on.

These people were now under Lila's absolute dominations. They could not ever BEGIN TO THINK OF REVOLT or of plans to replace the horror that was engulfing their last sureties of comfort—their last shreds of what we call rights—for the telaug beams of Lila's cronies and pet slaves and favorites, always about, would have instantly revealed even the slightest thought of treachery, and their reward for "squealing" would have been floods of indulgence in the form of stim, of women trained in stim-debauchery from their childhood on—or even the personal attentions of Lila and Yahveh, in this respect. Treachery could not have been repressed by a surface man, for every evil was here in Lila's constant indulgence of all her whims, rampant—and a normal man cannot help desiring some rights, some dignity, some virtue to which to cling with pride—somethng to hold as assurance that his life is not wholly a waste. But none of these things are allowed one under the domination of such as Lila Onderde was now fully become. To hold such thoughts was "treachery." Those who survived under Lila, assiduously cultivated a severity of mind, a thought discipline of unimaginable severity of refusal of virtue, of ferocity of lust for blood and death to anything that might threaten the supremacy of Lila Onderde—and Satan—as Lila masqueraded the helpless Yahveh.

AROUND Lila this mental attitude must always be "real," must be worn like one's clothes, and must be followed as the rule of conduct upon all occasions. Those who failed to alter their soul to fit Lila's nature—to fit it scrupulously by copying every observed activity of the High Priestess of Sin—those people died slowly and in the eyes of all, a lesson to the rest.

Let us look at one of the greater "feasts" held by these Satanists under the domination Lila Onderde has brought to the work of making Sin paramount on earth.

The hour of the feast has arrived, and about the great, gloomy rock chamber hand the decorations, nicely writhing in their niches from the wired stim currents flowing through their naked limbs.

The terrific ancient carvings on the walls, nicely polished by slaves, and new looking, but smoked and darkened again in places from the many fires of the recurrent Demon feasts—and every feast an orgy of blood-letting for the inverted pleasure senses of Lila and her cronies.

Scrabbling, crablike, the mighty body of Yahveh finds its horrible way across the stage in an awed silence of fear.—For many of the Satanists think he is the true and immortal Devid-God himself—and with good reason for many are his evil deeds done under Lila's constant control. Above, in her luxurious chambers, Lila sits at the great mech, controlling his tortured movements with the great ray, and augmenting the audience's awe with little diffuse stim beams so that the worships this thing, Yahveh, her tool. Yahveh takes his place on the great dais, his mighty, evilly twisted body becomes the center of the gathering, the focus of all eyes, the dominating background for all the writhing Hell that is to occur there today. Lila freezes his body in place with a shot of the epilepto ray that sets his great mutilated muscles in immobile position, and leaves the switch of the ray on until she has played her part in the program. Then she takes a last look in the mirror, her body twists sensuously as she postures her hips right and left in lewd suggestiveness—her slave girls dust her with powder, adjust about her waist the tight jeweled cincture that accents the curve of her hips and the smallness of her waist, set the green emeralds flaming at her wrists and ankles, place on her head the great polished wood mask that will proclaim her the Devil's chief hand-maid, touch up the rouge of her cheeks under the curling locks that cascade down her nude back and shoulders—and Lila undulates down the stairs and out to the great dais before the painfully frozen statue of living flesh that is the mighty slave—Yahveh—become now the living re-incarnation of Sathanas by Lila's subtle work.

Tonight was to be a greater indulgence in the art of torment for pleasure than any other previous, a greater let-down of the bars that hold life from becoming wholly evil— a greater display of sensual, mad excess of carnality.—For fortune was smiling on Lila Onderde—she was living to the full—and she knew how to enslave the senses of her following, how to give them what they wanted most. She knew her Devil-horde and was in the process of making them her devoted slaves entirely. Such were her thoughts.

As Lila writhes forward under the decorations, that include, among other horrifics, stuffed human figures, slave girls still hasten about their task of strewing straw about the floor, of setting all the places with many odd dishes peculiar to the feast, the blood goblets, the finger bowls filled with scented water—the sauces and condiments. The sulphuric perfumes alleged to be present were not so, but instead some very stimulating perfumes were brought for the occasion from the rare stores of unguents and scents of the ancients themselves. Some of these were of the type producing panurgic reactions in the male and nymphomania in the female.

The living decorations were like the statues brought to a strange and terrible activity by some fearful magic, by the terrific stimulation of sexual motions by the ancient life-energy force-flows.

The red lilies of this feast strewed the floor and stood in great vases wherever a place might be found for them, and about the black, shining body of Yahveh rested a great bank of the black lilies of death so dear to alleged black heart.

Lila pauses before she sweeps out to the center of the dais in her dance of prostration to the power of Sin—to speak for a moment to her chief advisor,—a scrawny, long-nosed and cunning little man who had been her father's chief stool-pigeon before her father's sudden demise. He had ingratiated himself with Lila by making her seizure of the reins less troublesome with some of her father's followers than she had expected.

"The feast has become the central point of our life, someway—the fools have taken up the worship of Satan more vigorously than ever before—it is your beauty and your wisdom which has made our power grow so greatly. Ah, Lila, you are a flame of Evil tonight. My old bones grow desirous with just the glimpse of you—and when you dance—I pray for the strength of youth again."

"You old liar—you would cut my throat in an instant if you thought you would benefit by it. But do not think I have not taken my precautions—besides who else would allow you the privileges I do? Are the gift coffers well laden, you old goat?"

"Filled to the brim with gifts for Sathanas, my queen. This business is one of our greatest sources of income. It pays better than taxes, in truth. The wizardry of your dupe, Yahveh, has made the fools actually believe in the flummery—actually think you have found the secret of becoming immortal. Twas a great stroke, your acquiring that fellow."

"Do not forget the power I have won with him, and get ambitious, my Crakon. You would not look so well as Yahveh does with your limbs all crushed like him—would you? Nor would you live through it, as he has?" Lila knew his thoughts, had a purpose in her speech.

CRAKON looked askance at Lila, for in truth he had had some ideas of trying to take over the mighty power she was building up with her shows of Sathans' worship—the terrific accumulation of wealth and curious stim-mech machines and other kinds of valuable and rare work of the ancients, which is the greatest value of the subterranean world. For the wild ones of the far caves could not be held without this kind of mental duping, without some sort of superstitious over-aweing of their wild combative nature—and would not have brought the rare old things into the city of Onderde without some such drawing card as the wild debauches with which she attracted them from their fastnesses—and with which she held their interest and satiated their sadistic savage appetites.

Flames were roaring now from a full hundred cooking fires about the walls, and over each revolved a spit, and on the spits were pieces of human flesh, the main delicacy of these feasts.

Lila now, her near nude, provocative body posturing in a thousand subtle movements suggestive of desire and its gratification, writhed out from the wings of the dais, and after a short ceremonial invocation to the black figure of Yahveh in the background

—lay full length before him, belly upward—for the altar of Satan is traditionally the nude body of the high priestess of the Dark God.

Now a processions of dishes for the feast were placed upon her gleaming white body, for the blessing of Sathanas, and the great figure of the giant black man, under the watch and control of several concealed ray-warriors—nodded its head gravely and ceremonially over each of these dishes—some of which were the nicely browned bodies of babies.

Now Lila rises and postures before the terrible mutilated figure of black strength, the "Devil Incarnate"—and begins the "dance of the She-Devil" which she is eminently fitted to portray.

That dance of a soul becoming the Devil's ecstatic property—that dance, for sheer wanton lust of the flesh, for sheer all out casting off of all spiritual and moral restraint (such as lingers in all surface men's equivalent performances) can give the mind a view into the true fiery lure of Hell.

A feature of the dance is the slaying of some poor slave, and his living heart cut from his body—Lila offering the pulsing heart to Satan as a reward for the giving of herself to him forever. Satan—(Yahveh under control by concealed ray-warriors) takes the heart from her hands and attempts to consummate the gift by taking the promised body of the She-Devil then and there. Lila, acting her part, feigns fear of the terrible strength and huge black fearfulness of the figure of Sathanas—retreats about the stage —with Sathanas in pursuit. The rest must be left to the imagination.

The dance of this blood-dabbled priestess of the Sabbath is the beginning of an orgy such as few men of normal mind ever see—and stay sane.

Picture for yourselves the audience, sprawling in a great crowd about the smoke vast chamber of vanished power and glory, their eyes drinking in the utterly savage scene. Then remember that this scene has taken place exactly the same since before we had a Santa Claus, since before the Egyptians had a Pharaoh, the same devil worship in the caves was old. True, Lila and her living Devil-God were an innovation—but an improvement, from the little, twisted peoples point of view. (And remember that the hypocritical evil of a Hitler is vastly more revolting to an honest mind than this out-and-out mad prostration before the spirit of evil. Also, remember that under Berlin some of these same hereditary devil races had a finger in that bloody Nazi pie—and conducted their own demon worship between spells of whispering demoniac advice into Hitler's ear—or debauching the Beast of Belsen into new furies of efforts to remove the life from every one he could get his hand upon.)

The minds of such creatures of today—who still exist in the endless labyrinth of the Elder World—have been for endless centuries under the absolute control of ray workers themselves more debauched than surface mind can imagine—have been shaped in a mold of inhuman thought forms by the powerful control beams of the telaug till reactions inconceivable to us have replaced forever every natural reaction within their minds. Such is hereditary evil—a ray-cultured mind fitted to the evil mold by century after century of clever, evil hands upon the ray controls about their young life. Generation after generation of children have been raised to think only evil in these Demoniac centers under earth. And, to give the underworld its just due—other centers of culture just as wholly good have for an age gone on with their struggle with these evil centers —and are our only hope against this evil still today—for surface man has developed no weapon to equal the antique ray—and shows no signs of doing so except radar.

Remember that both the good and the evil ray people have for ages had beneficial rays of great curative powers in their ignorant hands, and have, even today, when our technicals could have made some progress in understanding the antique science—not found a way of getting one bit of the medically beneficial-ray generator mech to the surface scientists. Remember, too, this could not be written did not good ray people keep off the "rods"—the wild devil ray of America.

LILA'S body, made apparently immortally healthy and so terribly and irresistibly beautiful by the application of Yahveh's wisdom as to the proper uses of the beneficial rays and healthful vibrants with which the ancient mansions abound—for when the ancients took to space—most of the heavy equipment had to be left behind—bound here by the necessity for the conservation of space in a long space voyage. Lila's body was the dominating motive of this carnival of fecundity in evil that was growing ever greater about the Palace of Onderde under Jerusalem. The continual employment of some hundreds of slaves expert with stim rays to cause the more prominent of her devotees to swoon with love for Lila, and their work and their wealth were all hers to command, as well as their bodies when she so chose. Lila walked always with her body radiant with a flood of stim rays from dozens of slaves appointed to her personal attendance in this way—and to look at her thus aflame with the terribly potent sexual synthetic nerve-impulses was to be forever her slave—unless one were a Yahveh of strength.

Behind Lila Onderde ever hovered the knowledge of the presence of Sathanas, apparently also the ecstatic slave of her pleasure—for did she not delight in showing his vast black body imprisoned within the metal walls of the healing mechanism—that body so twisted and infernal in appearance—that head that could only have come from a man with the noble lineage of the Elder Gods themselves—and was not Sathanas the outcast of Heaven?

But those terrible hands projected now from holes cut in the metal healing box to do certain tasks with ray controls of the milder kind that were placed there close to his reach—looked very strange and terrifying to Lila at times. And at times Lila knew that she was a thing lower than the slime of the sea bottom to have made of Yahveh what she had made of him. But there were always available many men to solace and to laugh away such thoughts for her.

Her servants of Evil were drawn now from the wide borders of the known world of that time—the known caverns—little men from the caverns under the dark jungles of Africa, great Zulus from the Witch Doctors kraals come to learn—men from the now for centuries degraded caverns below Olympus—come to see Lila Onderde the famous Witch who had captured and enslaved the very power of Evil in Person—Sathans himself. Her gold and power they talked about, and under her many ray-servants compelling stim impulses, in the ceremonies of the many Sataernalia they threw offerings of their own gold into the coffers placed beside the doorways or tossed as a more personal tribute about her body when it lay white and nude before the great black form of the motionless Yahveh, posed to represent Sathanas.

The terrible bacchanals with which their lavish tribute was rewarded were exhausting and completely enslaving to the devotees who were, when present, subjected to subtle brain influences from her skilled group of ray experts—who, by subtle and unperceived cuttings and hypnotically strong insertions of ray-impulses in brain centers—made of the conscious ego of the pilgrims not self-determining persons, but people who would thereafter be subject to certain irresistible weaknesses—could be controlled by those who knew what those weaknesses were. All this was the art of ray-rule which Lila had learned in the court of her father, and went on almost without conscious planning all the time—as part of the process of fastening forever the domination of Onderde rule upon these who had heretofore been subject to other powers now dead or vanquished by Lila's ever expanding armies at the frontier of her Empire.

These terrible bacchanals became, too, times when Lila reveled in her complete subjugation of Yahveh's nature to the reins of her will—times when she reveled in her power over all the natural instincts and desires of Yahveh's inner self. She heard the voice of this self, although Yahveh himself could not any longer, so long as the enslaving hook-up of the complex telaugment held him in its bondage. As Lila heard these natural wishes and thoughts of Yahveh—she habitually did exactly opposite to his wishes—knowing and hearing the resulting mental torment and taking pleasure in her ability to so torment the mighty Yahveh.

Thus it was to make his enslavement to her more complete that she had placed beside his metal prison the stim-organ and rays from it obeyed her wishes—her slightest whim, for Yahveh was but an instrument of her will—and not even truly conscious of his own thought—but only of hers. So it was that when Lila amused herself with a young male slave—or with the obsequious ambassador from some tribute-paying province —it was Yahveh's twisted hands that operated the stim upon them—that made the man desire Lila's beauty and Lila's body more than life. It was Yahveh's hands that with wizard proficiency adjusted the stim ray to the maximum potential bearable by the strong body of Lila—whatever the result to the less powerful bodies of her victims—for Lila was now a woman of great physical strength due to the constant use of the powerful growth rays under the wise Yahveh's mental supervision. It was Yahveh's wizardry which constantly provided Lila's bed and Lila's lovers with the mightiest possible pleasure—and it was Lila who enjoyed Yahveh's mental torment at these men who usurped his place at her side—for Yahveh was not conscious of his thoughts—and Yahveh had loved Lila when they were together what seemed such a long time ago.

But in truth he was becoming well weaned of desiring the beauty of Lila Onderde, the daughter of a line of sadistic Demoniacs. But it was his utter agony at the vile usage of his mighty talents and wisdom, placed on earth expressly to serve the future of all men—and usurped by this evil incubus which diverted all his wisdom to the utter servitude of Evil ignorance.

It was this protesting small voice* from the once dominant Lahveh which Lila most enjoyed—for Lila was not a full blown dero—and the dero is the cause and servant of all evil everywhere—Lila was now fully come into her inheritance from her mad ancestors—and such always go by opposites.

FOOTNOTE—*As better men than I have before observed—as Oscar Wilde has written—"For all men kill the thing they love—the coward does it with a word—the brave man with a sword"—and we all know there is vital truth in that poem when we read it—but very few men ever understand completely just what truth is so fully expressed. Nor why it is true and vital—nor of whom it is true, for certainly not all men do kill the thing they love—yet it somehow rings true when we read it . . . Those who do kill the thing they love, or destroy it utterly by such enslavement as Lila practiced—or by ignorant and savage words slay the love they have aroused—do so BECAUSE THEY ARE (sometimes temporarily) UNDER THE INFLUENCE—ARE ROBOT TO DETRIMENTAL ENERGY FLOWS WHICH REPLACE AND OVERWHELM THE NATURAL ELECTRIC FLOWS FROM THE CELL BATTERIES OF THE MIND WHICH ARE THE MATERIAL OF THOUGHT. These detrimental flows are opposite in nature to the natural integrant flows of energy in the mind of man. But some men are hereditarily apt to become electrically sun-polared, inductive of sun energy mentally—and the integrant flows of the mind become overwhelmed by these sun-sourced disintegrant flows—sometimes permanently—just as a compass points forever north—so does the compass of the gray matter of their mind forever point toward destruction—disintegrance instead of integrance—giving what the ancients knew as "dero" and what is today called in the caverns the "rod" which is the same word as dero but inverted.

The knowledge of the nature of this evil of sunplanet life Yahveh Jehovah was now plumbing to the depths under the domination Lila Onderde's now terrible will—a will from mind cells that steadily inducted direct from the vast reservoirs of the disintegrate sun itself the will—the electric impulse to disintegrate and destroy (same word) due to their inhereited weakness to become so sun-polared when subjected to electric flows from sun polared mechanisms—and there are many such machines of ray in the caverns which have been used for centuries to bring sunlight direct over the conductive penetrative beams down through the rock above the caves into the darkness. It is a pitiful fact that Evil of the foulest kind should have resulted from man's first clever use of the conductive ray magic of the ancients to bring the sunlight and cheer of the surface down into the dark abandoned homes of the vanished Elder race.

So it was that Lila projected regularly the image of Yahveh's twisted, enslaved body before her worshipping throngs of her devotees—or made him pose in person as the Devil Sathanas—or made love to his unprotesting body as a part of the ritual of Sin.

Lila controlled thus all his reactions, dictated his thought, made of the helpless giant a plaything and tool before the degenerate mob of her "subjects"—so that all might see that she controlled the "Devil" body and soul, and was, therefore, greater than the "Devil" and likewise an "immortal" worthy of the same or greater worship.

So it was that the Legend of the Devil and his twisted black body became a part of Satanism everywhere—and so it has been that a woman has ever been his chief priestess—and the Witch his instrument of power everywhere—through the custom set by Lila for the centuries of darkness that followed her destruction of the gift of a Messiah from the Elder race direct to man.

LILA'S own mortal prostration before the pleasure of doing evil was now as complete as was Yahveh's before her power.

Under these conditions the dominion of Evil grew steadily, the borders of Lila's dominions grew through the caverns, ever southward—for the northways were mostly blocked by lava flows from Etna and Vesuvius and other causes made the North the land of no return.

The numbers of her armies became past counting or management—and like the Juggernaut that was Rome, she found herself astride an automatically increasing monster of power which no stupidity or cruelty of her seemed great enough to harm.

Her generals stood before her in court ceremonies by the hundred, crowding even those mighty God-chambers built by the Dead Great for just such purposes as Lila had invertedly adopted. Reports took long hours of precious time from her pleasures which grew daily more demanding and more terrible of consequence for that unit of which all such strengths are built—the humble working man.

The circuses, held monthly and which were a kind of sop thrown by Lila to this humble brick of her vast edifice of Empire, just as were the Roman circuses—were in truth vastly more savage and entertaining than any unstimmed imagination of Roman emperor ever created.

There were ever more lavish as her power and her extravagance grew in unison. Under Jerusalm the mighty spectacles of gladiatorial combat, of beasts mangling young girls, of slaves sacrificed to stranger fates than ever were dreamed up for any Caesar in any arena—went on, and the vast chambers of the by-gone great under Jewry filled again with life—so that the caverns swarmed now constantly with caravans, with marching troops, with trundling antique war-machines—with captives led in chains to their slavery or to death in the arena—and with wagons laden wth that strange loot of stim ray mech and weird weapon rays which any modern scientist would give his right arm for at any time even today—especially today.

The frontiers grew so that even Lila could not visualize or remember what was hers and what was another's—and in truth few argued with the armies which were equipped and sent out by Yahveh's enslaved wizardry.

The caverns are far vaster, area for area, than the surface world—and lie in tiers, or levels, and to remember upper Abyssinia from "level eight" Abyssinia from "lower" Abbyssinia was too much for Lila and for many another cavern monarch—so that the saying "Anything can happen in the caverns" was as true of Lila's holdings as was it of anywhere ever. Tier on tier of ancient factories and weird, enigmatic machinery, of dried-up synthetic-sun-ray gardens—of great mansions, and level on level of empty cities—all contains much of the left-behind stores and riches of the Elder race where they had abandoned it in their precipitate flight so long ago.

What to do with the vast influx of slaves, of wagon loads of loot, became a vast circle of merchants laboring at totting up their ledgers for Lila Onderde's accounts.—Of endless store-rooms, (empty since the last Giant God's loaded space craft had taken off from earth into the eternal night of space.) that were now filled with the vast loot flowing in steadily from her warring armies' steady victories. Lila's tactical experts, under Yahveh's Elder race technique, were invincible.

The whole vast system of Empire became a top-heavy fabric of war and loot and business untended to—just as Empires other than this dark cess-pool of Onderde became in those days.

Ever the true soul of Yahveh shrank from the terrible growth of Evil which Lila had fecundated and brought into being upon his unresisting body—by his helplessly servile hands delivered of the womb of war and lust—taught to viler usages,—taught by his helpless mind to be more cunning in evil than any other.

Yahveh's body had now been largely repaired and much of the structural damage had been replaced by new ligaments and sinews under the continual growth of the healing rays of the chamber in which Lila had habitually kept him imprisoned. Twisted and evil of appearance his body was, but it was once again a strong servant of his mind—when and if he should again win control of his own thoughts.

He did not think much about this healing, only shifting his position sometimes when he had been unable so to do before—for no thought was of his own origination. he thought only upon command—and then only on the subject commanded.

Lila noted this return to full mobility in the use of his limbs, and thought not greatly about it for Yahveh had ceased to think greatly about anything and she had no cause to think of him any more than about one of her own hands, or feet.

Now, too, the body of Lila Onderde was fully developed from the girlish curves which Yahveh had known, into the fulness of ripe womanhood, and her legs into the grasping musculature which such busy legs should have. Her breasts were fair white mountains of voluptuous growth from the effects of the ever-flowing stim rays and beneficial growth rays pointed out to her by Yahveh's unwilling but obedient mind. Her skin was as soft and smooth as the hide of a new-born puppy from the soft, healthy, never-weary flesh underneath and the sleek oiled surface of it was ever alive with rippling vitality from treatment by the clever ray uses which no one on all earth but only Yahveh knew. Truly he was her greatest treasure—and, likewise, as was in line with her dero nature—the least appreciated or rewarded member of her court.

HER arms were two smooth white pythons which few could resist desiring, particularly as a hundred slaves swept over the court with stim rays cleverly mixed with thought-record compulsion to love of Lila Onderde, the Empress.

Her height was now far greater than any ordinary man's from the constant use of the growth rays, but the inherited evil of her mind was such that she did not grow mentally but remained for that same reason of inherited stupidity only the same selfish and sensuous female she had always been, though her constant hearing and use of Yahveh's thought concealed this and made her seem the wisest of the wise and the most cunning of all her evil crew. The ruthlessness and cleverness thus acquired by her mind was enhanced, too, by its great acquisition of experience in handling of men and the handling of the intricate and difficult machines of the ancients, under Yahveh's tutelage.

Clad in many glittering jewels of the master workmanship which are only found in the cavern world, hung with the plumes of ostriches, her hair dusted with the raw gold dust of Africa or adorned over its sleek curled blackness with great pearls from the far east, around her neck a great string of emeralds and her whole sensuous body crawling under the fair soft skin with those muscles which continuous boudoir exercise gives to woman under the potent rays of the ancient wisdom which give such ability through the night that there is no other woman equal to one used to such rays—Lila Onderde was the greatest and most beautiful harlot in all the world of that time. Vast were her conquests, and no vile roman Empress ever equalled her debaucheries, her cruelties, or her conquests.

And Yahveh, his inner-self forever protesting in Lila's ears, lay within his confining metal chamber and worked ever supinely for what he most despised and hated—for the often as not slew him in the morning to be well rid of his future worship and the hypnotic trance of love in which such stimulative rays leave the ordinary man when first under their influence.

Too, she knew that it would not do to have too many people privy to her secrets, that anyone who knew her method of enslaving Yahveh could with aid do likewise to her, and she had no wish to be so enslaved.

When she took such a man, she could not resist showing him her Yahveh and his prostration to her will, and she could not resist making the unwilling Yahveh stim their union with all his superhuman ability with such ray mech—for her pleasures were not near so great except she so used him during her play.

Yet that very use of him would give away to one well used to the various telaug mech the secret of the method of such enslavement. Knowing that it would be a stupid man indeed who would not dream of winning dominion over all her power and wealth in the same way—it became a habit for her to examine her partner's thoughts each morning carefully, and lucky was he whom she was soft enough to allow to go his way after such a night. Many she had slain out of hand, sometimes by herself subtly with poison, others very pleasantly and longwindedly by her torturers in the same room where Yahveh still lay within his prison chamber—others she kept on hand imprisoned in dungeons for further uses of similar kind.

The next night she chose another lover from among the young men and young slaves who flowed through her palace in streams from the far borders on missions, officers, prisoners—emissaries—there were always about the palace many eligible young men for what she had in mind when she looked at a man. And wily indeed did many of them become in avoiding the eyes of Lila Onderde.

This torrent of bloodshed grew somewhat less as the private dungeons became near-filled with the available young men.

* * * * *

A loud slapping noise brought me—Dick Shaver—back from that world where Lila Onderde held forth in her mad welter of too great prosperity and indulgence— back to sanity and the sweet face of Nydia working over the ancient mech where the brittle thought-record had broken. She grinned at me, saying—"She was an old bat, wasn't she? That Messiah was my idea of a real Messiah, too, till she got hold of him. How I would like to get her under my ray just once."

And a savage expression crossed my sweet Nydia's face so that I realized that she was the child of a cruel and terrible life, and would thoroughly enjoy killing off one of the world's curses such as Lila Onderde. And I loved her for that ability on her face.

"I hope you get that old record patched, for I would hate never to know whether

Yahveh got his freedom again or not. What do you think?"

"I know, Dick! I've got it back together, but if that time-indication by which the record makers indicated the passage of time has been balled up by the break, you will never know.how long Yahveh was under her spell—and you may never see his release if I have had to remove too much of this cracked section of tape. Here we go again, lean back before you pass out" . . .

* * * * *

ABRUPTLY the curtain closed over my consciousness. I was again a disembodied spirit within the mighty borings of the holding of Lila Onderde. Within the ancient, stinking torture chamber, where Yahveh still lay within the prison healing chamber where he had lain under Lila's mastery for I will never know how many years. As I adjusted my mind to this condition of being just the sensing of the breathing of the mighty Yahveh, just the seeing of the stained walls and the dank smell of blood and passed agony that was this place—I saw a thin black hand, far off in Lila Onderde's lavishly decorated boudoir, stealing so silently along the wall. I was seeing and hearing all this through the mighty augmentation of Lila's onto Yahveh's sleeping thoughts where she lay, far off on her great couch of red silk, under the huge ben-ray lamps, her eyes closed, her breathing even, her body nude in the heat of the place whose ventilation system is certainly not what it was when the ancients built it.

Above her innumerable barbaric evidences of her riches, golden plaques on the walls, coffers of jewels and ornaments hang open spilling their contents at the side of the vast room. On the floor great furry skins, polar bear skins brought from the far north none might know how today, tiger hides across the chairs ebony gleam, hangings of the patient embroidery of that time—silken and bright with golden threads, with scarlet flowers and a great glistening leaves of silk threads—and on a small stand a dried human head with long yellow hair of some notable which she had had so preserved to commemorate some triumph over the dead man. And beside her sleeping form that thin black arm, sliding so softly along the great keyboard of the mechanisms by which she held her terrible grip upon the might of Yahveh, the son of the Lost Gods on Earth. All this I could see, as it were through the mentally enslaved Yahveh's eyes that were yet but ragged sockets in his terrible and wise face that seemed to look awfully at me where I was but a sensing upon the heavy air—and to Yahveh, not yet born. And whether Yahveh was watching the sliding black arm, and how such an accurate record of events that could hardly have been recorded as they happened was made, I will never know—though Nycea has explained it to me as the custom of the wise of the caverns, to make records of their own thought about such events soon after they happened—and that this particular record must have been made by Yahveh himself in compliance with the custom of keeping such records. But, however, it was done in the far past from which that record came into Nydia's choice library of such Mentalia, it was terribly real and actually happening as that thing, pitifully scarred blackchild's arm slid steadily along the great God-keyboard of the teliplex multi-aug mech of Yahveh's electric chains, and it was terribly important to someone that the steady sleep breathing of that Demoness Lila Onderde go on and on, and in the air was a faint picture of her dreams from the great augmentation, which was perhaps Yahveh's memories of the horrors that such dreams were to him, making him act out their terrible details in actual occurrence into life's terrible reality.

And the dream was now of the time far off when she had walked in the metal mimc garden and the young, unmutilated body of Yahveh, the beautiful young God, had walked beside her, and I knew that somehow Yahveh had aroused that dream in her by suggestion, and was cunningly using her memory to keep her harpy nature enslaved in sweet, sleeping memories of the past—and suddenly that thin little black arm above had reached its goal and there came a sharp snap and the picture flashed into darkness! But not in the torture chamber, there was still light, and no consciousness of Lila Onderde there to prison the might of Yahveh against his will.

And now within the metal walled chambering prison began a terrible struggle, and the great black limbs lashed out again and again against the locked metal doors, but to no avail, he could not break that master worked metal of the lock. And even as his new used limbs wearied of the struggle against his bonds—into the dank blood-smelling place stole a thin little black girl, some negro slave girl of the palace who had conceived and carried out her plan of vengeance against some remembered terrible cruelty of Lila Onderde's. And there was still the thing to be finished and on her face; her thin, lined little face that was yet beautiful with that thin nosed Arab beauty that is sometimes the negroe's. Those pouting young flower red lips parted in agonized haste against the time when chance shall waken the Demoness sleeping above against her and against the mighty prisoned Demon himself. Such is the girl's thought—yet there is in her thought a still greater understanding and wonder of what this mighty twisted negro may really be whom Lila keeps forever locked and chained with so many kinds of bonds against the use of his will. Swiftly her feet whisper across the stone and swiftly her hands fit the thin old key she has stolen from Lila's perfume table, from among the long box full of gauds and glittering jewels upon that many scented place of her endless toilettes.

Swiftly the thin hands fit the key to the lock. At last the wised Demon . . . (whom she does no know is a Demon of right and sanity—hoping only that he will help her against Lila) is loosed in the stronghold of Evil where he has been Lila's slave.

THE terrible mutilated body twists slowly out, and falls to the floor, and lies for a time still there upon the floor. Now with the will of him driving those limbs that are so fearful in their twisted shapelessness, like the trunks of great trees grown on peaks in the ever-winds of the high places—those twisted limbs writhed and shuddered and held at last the great scarred torso aloft under the lash of his will.

He was at last out of the metal box where so many vile years of slavery have kept him, and for an instant as he totters on his feet, the long, beautiful powerful hand of the black God touches the thin negro girl-child's head and he whispers—"Why, little one, why do you do this for me?"

"Because Lila Onderde is worse than a devil to me, and you many not be the devil that she is to me. Kill her, and be free. She has always boasted you are her slave. Kill her swiftly before she awakes, or I will be killed for setting you free."

Those soft black eyes of the child that were yet somehow hard and bright with hate glared up into Yahveh's empty eye sockets. Somehow a tear found it's way out of the horrible socket scars of Yahveh's face, for Yahveh was hurt that a child should have at last saved him from his succubus and given him his will again—only for hate, and not for love of him or for understanding—but only because she reasoned him to be the lesser of two evil things.

And Yahveh had no longer time, nor did his movement really cease as this moment's interchange explained the occurrence to him.

Slowly, so terribly slowly, his limbs found their way into the unaccustomed movements, and twistedly his vast body teetered across the floor and found the stairs and clambered upward like a vast black crab upon his hands and knees. And behind him came whispering the feet of the little vengeful black maid who had freed him, for she knew that in all the palace there was for her now only protection in that broad back and those blind eyes and terrible beautiful hands of Yahveh the mighty—but to her he was the Devil himself, and she feared him mightily. She shuddered at every horrible motion of his twisted limbs in their agony of effort—but still she followed, for had her father not been a mighty hunter, and a brave warrior—there was no fear would conquer her! And Yahveh was thankful for those whispering bare feet at his back for the girl had eyes that would serve his purpose did be find a need.

Thus the terrible climb up through the spiral stairs from the dungeon, the black, twisted limbs writhing with muscles that contracted without moving anything, being cut —yet healed in every way that they could be healed—the terrible iron will that still lived in the giant godling drove him, drove those limbs that were so horrible in their shapelessness, like the trunks of great trees grown in the wind on mountain peaks. Those limbs twisted on to the upper level where the chambers of Lila were, and writhed and tottered and held again the terrible scarred torso erect—and now with some touch of their former swiftness the great black arms reached out and touched the black maid on the shoulder while he steadied himslf and took his point from her directing steps, and followed where she led—for she knew him well that he was blind.

Through the vast beautiful halls of the place that had been built by his own father's people—had been dirtied and disfigured by the centuries of later people that had spawned Lila Onderde—that crablike, skittering progress of the son of the Gods went—past the terrific beauty of the ancient sculptures that are so much vaster in their wonder of human form than any man can grasp.—Like a crippled giant ape under those beautiful stone eyes of the Promethean figures that were the statues of his forefathers.—A monster from the depths of some hell he seemed—this mighty man who had been gifted to the human race to save it from the sun "de" if such saving were possible—this mighty man of wisdom who had been so terribly degraded by those same humans he had been born to save.—On toward the big cedar-wood door that had been fitted to Lila's own rooms. And somehow the spirit that is just revenge walked rightly with the little negro girl and the crippled giant, the child leading the blind, tottering giant, her face now a mask of fear—of horror at her temerity in entrusting her life to the protection of this giant who was, it seemed a tottering weakling. She was a dead girl, her thoughts kept on and on—she was as good as dead—and long and painful would be her death under Lila's rays of pain.

A cruder body no primitive artist had ever conceived than this that bore the noble head of the blind Yahveh on toward vengeance, onward through the long halls toward his meeting with Lila Onderde once again face to face after all these years of his mind's prostitution. And on that blind face burned a rage that no God's face ever bore before, for Yahveh was close to madness from long domination by the mad Lila.

NOW at last he stood before the door of the apartments where Lila Ondrede slept, having dismissed her many women so that she might sleep in peace, and having kept the little black girl merely because the girl wished instead to play.—Kept her to make sure that no one should disturb her. Had she not only last week beaten her half to death for failing to hasten on an errand! Certainly she would not be disturbed!

Yahveh stood now before the great cedar-wood door, and his fingers pressed the shoulder of the little black girl in question, and she reached up her fierce little face and spoke one word of assent softly to him. And soft as that word was, it was yet a harsh sound to hear from any child.

Yahveh summoned his strength for one moment, then set his great shoulder to the door and it crashed inward in pieces and he fell inward before the startled, wakened, suddenly blazing eyes of Lila Onderde—he fell in upon her, staggering and feeling with his mighty twisting hands for her before she could again whelm him with the telaug rays with which she had controlled him so long.

And Lila rolled swift as an otter across the great bed away from him but the little negro maid shouted to Yahveh and pushed him toward her, for she wished to live, and there was now no hope but this great blind cripple.

Lila slid swift around the groping hands and toward the door, but even faster than her flying feet were the desperate feet of the cunning, vengeful little negro, and Lila was tripped by one thin black shin and fell full length.

And at the sound of her large soft body falling to the floor, Yahveh gave one humping leap upon the sound, and his hands found that soft form they had once fondled, and slid swiftly upward toward that traitorous throat, and the white, sleek throat now was soft again under his hands as it was of old when he fondled her unwilling before she took to using every night a new youth. And the sleek white hide purpled swiftly under his terrible fingers, and Yahveh did not waste time, but twisted that now strong neck brutally right and left to break her spinal bones—but the strength of the ray was in her, and Yahveh's muscles were no longer present where they should be. And they strove and wrestled there on the floor and Lila's breath came in great gasping screams and then came not at all—but still she threw her body this way and that like a great white snake, so supple was she from the strengthening growth ray's effects. And still the black and awful thing that was Yahveh clung to the white thrashing beauty of her body, and slower and slower was the twining of the sinuous white body about his black mighty arms—and the shining black eyes of the little maid bent now savagely searching over his shoulder and blind head watching Lila's empurpled face for the sign that means death. And at last she grew still, and moved no more, and Yahveh kept still pressing his fingers inward and would not stop till death himself should pry him loose from this horror that had consumed his life-gift to the future of man.

And softly the negro slave girl put back the pieces of the cedar door and attempted to set things to right in some thought of finding a way to conceal the deed till thought could be taken what to do next.

And as feet sounded without, Yahveh, his blind face wet with the sweat of the evil and terrible struggle—let now loose his hold and flung himself aloft and across the room to the great mech by Lila's bed, and his swift hands found there the switches and the bright light of the telaug blazed up into his blind eyes and the sight that was there given him into his mind's eyes of perception was not good!

Long and white her twisted body lay there before him, and her dead breasts wet with the bloody froth from her mouth awry—so undeniably finished she was—the deadly beauty she had exercised to the detriment of all men—this Lila who had betrayed and ruined him. And Yahveh's heart was warm with the knowledge that the deed was done! Now, his hands flexed above the keys of Lila's mighty old weapon mech like an organ player long denied his music. And now down from Lila's place at that great mech flashed his ray of vengeance upon the whole evil court where they were gathered waiting their usual unmentionable obeisance upon the appearance of Lila Onderde. And even as Lila's master ray flashed death terribly down upon the evil court, Yahveh was thinking that all the things he had planned and wanted for men lay there with her dead body, for within him dwelt now no desire to labor for the men of earth.

And even as he fought against the answering bolts of death from Lila's dying warriors—Yahveh's mighty voice—(that they, some of them, remembered with tremblings from the time when he had slain so many of them)—Yahveh's dreadful voice cursed a great curse that was heard by accidental ray-conductive even up in Jerusalem.—And the curse was heard and understood—and all those who had slain Jesus and wrecked his work thought that it was that God, whom Jesus had proclaimed, somehow now suddenly returned and the meaning they heard was this: "May this doing ye have done to all my work with you be upon your head forever—for Yahveh strives for you no more."

And even as he slew terribly all that crew that has festered and grown fat upon his slave work for Lila Onderde—plans were vaguely heard from the records which were his thinking—and those plans were to find some ancient craft of space within the labyrinths of caves and find his way toward the path his forefathers had taken.

And whether the Messiah was killed in the vengeance he visted on the Sycophants of Onderde or whether he did repair some ancient ship and abandon earth to the fate it seem d to him to deserve— we will never know, for . . .

*   *   *   *   *

Again came that slapping sound in my ears, and again I snapped back to welcome consciousness out of the spell of that awesome vengeance of the cripple giant upon the evil that had robbed all men of the ancient wisdom.

And as Nydia's sweet face bore toward me her kiss, I swore a great oath that men should hear aright the story of the true Messiah. So it is, and you have heard, nor sordidness nor futility nor awkwardness, nor anything that was there have I left out purposely.

And Nydia, hearing my thought, bore with her kiss to me the thought—"And somehow, Dick, we shall complete his work—for death must have claimed him or life on earth would today be vastly different and not the thing of frustration and futile circling that it is now."

"We may never complete his work, Nydia"—I murmured—"but we may at least try to set men's feet back on the way to wisdom and logic such as the Elder race has left us here in these records. We can try to travel the direction that race pointed. And may the lffe of Yahveh prove ever an example if only because of its frustration!"

— To be cont nued next issue —

WINGS IN THE NIGHT

By Richard S. Shaver

AND I looked into his eyes and saw there a man from forests now made into lumber piles, and with him I wept for our earth that is always made less than it must be.

I saw his people not. I saw his city, empty, and the small brightness of his own courage facing life—without forest and without people.

And I put my hand on his small back to comfort him, for I understood what man had done to him. And my hand felt there the wing stubs, and they were fledgling wings, and I knew that the men of his race had once been winged.

Of the lost people of Mexico, (Yucatan) I thought, who like others have not been honored with inclusion in the small immaterial reckonings of history. And the immense past I saw vast outlined against the small decreasing present, when his fellows flitted among the giants and the trees, a brother race to the sons of the Elder race. Or soared, more likely, above those trees that towered above Ygdrasil when it was small and but one among many.

Here he had come, to this place under Chicago, why or how I did not know, and it did not matter. What mattered was that steadily man destroys all that he touches, as he has destroyed his forests, his game, and his friends—like the small descendant of the once numerous winged race—like this man's race was once destroyed and now he did not much care for life. Even as I did not care for it, even as I wondered why one struggles on for man, his brothers, when they do not understand what is happening to them and why there is such terrible need for understanding.

Of these people who are spoken of in Mexico and South America with awe and fear and reverence, the people of the caverns, who can not bother with modern man except sometimes to do him a favor or a mischief. And there were fledgling wings upon his shoulders, and that tells a man much of the past.

Man once was winged, and this small relic of that time sat there and talked with me, to tell me of the lumber piles, and. what had happened to his life, and how he had been sent here as a curiosity—and to prove to us that men once more winged even as the stories say.

And I thought of the homes to be built of the lumber from the forests that had been stripped from over his head, leaving him and his wing stubs exposed at last to blind men's eyes, and how each family in those homes will be a family not knowing that among those trees had dwelt a man who had even yet the stubs of wings upon his back to prove that man was once winged. At least *one* race of man had wings! And I thought of all the other far echoing truths about their past that the white human termites within those homes of the lumber piles would also not know or believe if they were told—and with the small Indian, I wept, and he wept too; for he knew that blowing across the land of man was a withering wind, and the homes to be built would be again empty ruins filled only with that wind's shrill lonesome bickering with itself. Those homes built of the lumber of his destroyed forest that he loved would not even stand intact until that lumber had rotted away—but would be cut down again, even as his trees had been cut down.

And I turned over to go to sleep, but *she* said: "LISTEN!"

And I listened, and heard that wind across the roof, empty and alone, and I knew that my house too would soon be a ruin among ruins, and the wind only would remain.

I thought of my friends struggling with emptiness in the night time, filling me with the sad truths that must be written or men will never know, and I knew they were my only friends upon the earth who understand—my only real friends upon all earth.

So I got up to write about the little "savage" with the wing stubs so prominent upon his back, and the great hurt spirit sticking out of his bright human eyes, for if I did not take care of the work I would have no friends, and the wind across the roof would inherit my own lonesome howling spirit the sooner, so much sooner.

About the vanished forest home, and the little man with stubby wings who had retreated from the saw mill into the caves and there came north, and now was talking to me about it all—and wondering with me why men were not more, why they never did understand and do what they must do or perish forever.

And together we wrote this, because men must do things that way or do nothing very soon. But he has been destroying himself for so very long, and still there are more and more of them.

But then there are more ants, too. But is it important?

Are we important unless we do *more* about being so. Must we build houses of wood? Must we insist that men never had wings? Must we be incredulous of all that our mind does not know of the past. Must we fail to learn now to live with each other and grow toward a fit life? Must we be modern men, destroying each other?

The wind said yes!

But the spirit in the eyes of the winged man said—"Brother!"

CONCERNING
MR. PALMER'S LETTERS
AND
MR. SHAVER'S INERTIA

By Robert Kidwell

Foreword:

IT IS my extreme pleasure to be able to thank Mr. Palmer and Mr. Shaver for their kind cooperation in the discussion of the *Shaverian Hypothesis*: I hope they will accept my appreciation and realize that my following remarks are all in the interest of rendering an otherwise dull and uninteresting dissertation a little more interesting.

First, I desire to thank Mr. Palmer especially for calling to my attention the discovery of intensified cosmic radiation within the earth; I shall remember it and give careful consideration to all substantiating evidence. It was a great surprise to me, and I still cannot say whether I agree; it does, however, support my contention that if Mr. Shaver's *Supermen* do exist, they also will be affected by it, fully as much as we.

Second, I desire to register a protest concerning his interpretation of some of my words, requesting his pardon for not having clarified them sufficiently; in this I shall attempt to remedy the situation.

IN THE "Shaverian Hypothesis" I made the statement that the letters "J", and "W" were created only to aid in decreasing the growing complexity of our spoken and written languages. As an occasional rebuttal, certain replies were made. I should like to clarify my own words and attempt an answer to Mr. Palmer and, a little later, to Mr. Shaver.

In the paragraph referred to, it was meant that the sounds of letters would most certainly have changed, regardless of stassis of the written letter; then, too, the written symbol is probably based upon some long-forgotten language: having progressed to certain sounds, these symbols were then borrowed by other nations using different combinations and degrees of sounds. In place of changing the spoken, they naturally changed the written language for congruity.

Words of more recent origin have been taken from languages which have lost the original prononciation, and their ideographs could not possibly bear any subtle meaning; they have all been Romanticized when taken into English.

Does written Chinese, Japanese, Aramaic, Arabic, Egyptic or another group of symbols have any obscure meaning when read with the Shaverian alphabet? These symbols remain almost completely unchanged through aeons of time; yet, as in China, their pronunciation may differ so much that, although their written tongue may be readily understood by any who can read Chinese regardless of language, neighboring dialects have almost no words in common.

Why should not the older words contain letters which mean certain things? Many of them have come from the Greek language, others from Latin; both were based more or less upon the Phoenician adaptation of the Egyptian symbols into an alphabet, and the Egyptian, Greek, and Latin languages were Indo-Aryan in origin. The ancient Egyptian language was not too difficult from Greek, though the symbols used to portray that language were so completely different that only with the discovery of the Rosetta Stone could they be read; hey sill cannot be pronounced, even as a dialect of Greek.

It is suggested that the *Mechano*, upon which so many suppositions have been based, might be better investigated as *mechanikos;* why not apply the Shaverian alphabet to Greek? For example, have Mr. Shaver read *dynamis* and *paranoia.*

Apply the Shaverian alphabet to Latin; it is quite well-known that Latin was a well-developed language derived from various dialects of the Villanoven, and possibly partly from the Terramaren, branch of Indo-Aryan, though there were many important additions by other languages.

It has been offered as a scientific opinion that the present alphabet evolved by simplification from the polysyllabic symbols of more ancient ones, primarily Egyptian hieroglyphics, and that Latin was possibly the phonetic translation into the thereto unsymbolized words.   While newly coined words are more frequently being based upon older root words by proper addition of approved prefixes, is it not rather remarkable that more of the English—and German—language is not literally definitive?

As for "J" and "Y", you are quite right in calling me down, Mr. Palmer;   I protest, however, their use in such a sense.   Originally, "I", "J", and "Y" were "I", which was both vowel and consonant.   Proof is always beyond our reach, but it seems to be current belief that we English have retained the "I" as a vowel, given its consonant sound to "Y", but write it as "J", using "Y" in writing newer words coined since the change.   There are, of course, many exceptions, but so much fewer than would seem to be true that they evoke astonishment.

"W", as was stated, is just a double-"U", not a very old letter in itself, but the representative of a very old diphthong.   Like the other three mentioned, it has evolved from older uses, generally following an understandable pattern.   Thus a double-"U" would possibly remain a double-"U", or a repeated "U", until replaced; what, however, would be the difference?   What would be more natural than giving the usurping symbol the same sound, if possible, or at least, the same use, the same meaning?

IT IS quite true that I committed a serious blunder in my use of words, for the uses of such letters would retain that which is present—perhaps altogether changed and substituted—letters represent.

One of your statements in particular, Mr. Palmer, shocked me no little—that you, an extremely educated man, should refer to other books as "red-herrings"!   While I do not make this statement as a personal opinion, you can well imagine what others call—"Amazing Stories."

You are undoubtedly correct in your hypothesis that these symbolically literal meanings can be applied to other very old languages; but whereas Mr. Shaver—and you—seem to believe they are devolved from a superior, world-wide language formerly existing; it is more generally the opinion, though not accepted as a theory because of absense of proof, that such coincidences (and the word is used respectfully) are but natural, as natural as it is for primitive peoples to carve in stone or wood the form they desire to portray, the thought they wish to convey; as naural as it is for those forms to degenerate, or devolve or evolve, into the most striking, descriptive, and impressive lines which suggest, without unnecessary detail, the same thing.

In other words, the "T" mentioned which might actually be the reason for the definite meaning of integration in many older words, and more coincidentally in more recent words; it is, however, bordering upon the ridiculous and even insanity to assume that the man who discovered this key (if it be the true key) for which science has been seeking so long is right when he proceeds further and, without any scientific proof— or, if any, "proof" twisted to get his specific meaning—declares to the world that it is the remnant of a superior culture of which science has never been able to discover more than a trace.

Although Mr. Shaver has done nothing new, he has stumbled upon something very interesting, as can be seen when it is considered that "T" could very well have devolved, or developed, from the far more complex symbol, or picture, of a tree.

It is not definitely known, nor has very much attempt been made to conjecture, how the "D" originated; but that does not mean its connection with the meaning Mr. Shaver attributed to it is not naturally true; yet why conclude—equally without proof —that it devolved from a "superior" language?

There has been something very peculiar noticed, however, which might be of interest to Mr. Shaver and his supporters; it is suggested that they consider the similarity between the Greek "delta" and the pyramids of Egypt; Greece did have intercourse with the Egyptians, and so did the Phoenicians.

This could be one of the reasons why Mr. Shaver has met so frequently with so many failures—and why not?   As stated before, there are few rules to which there are no exceptions.

Incidentally, sir, I am quite embarrassed by your reference that my "hypothesis" or some parts of it upsets the "applecart of science": one of the main reasons I wrote it was to uphold science.   —but why should you defend it in my place?   I was—mistakingly, it seems—under the impression that "orthodox" science, personified by its devotees, would be even more upset were it compelled to include all of Mr. Shaver's hypotheses.

Mr. Shaver and you have asked for a controversial argument to his hypothesis concerning inertia; I hope you will both consider this, for I do believe that Mr. Shaver has committed some very obvious errors in physics, which I was compelled to correct in high-school.

MR. SHAVER, in your theory on inertia, you made this statement: "Here on Earth's surface we have never had the opportunity of observing a weightless object—." On this you based certain conclusions.

With some of those conclusions I must concur, but many of the others are quite different from scientific opinions; indeed, scientific conclusions are changing so rapidly that not even a scientist can keep up with them—either yours or their own. The aforementioned statement is one with which I must disagree.

One hundred pounds on earth will have a certain mass; on the moon, however, it will possess about sixteen pounds in weight, but the very same mass. Thus we conclude that while mass is independent of gravity, weight is the force exerted by it under the influence of any acceleration, including gravity. Mass is, true, a property of matter; but weight is an effect of matter—a force which is dependent upon mass. All one has to do to remove weight from an object is to take away gravity. I can easily, by waving my magic wand, remove all gravity from any small, free object named; this can anyone else do: we just drop it.

Do you take scientists for complete fools, Mister Shaver? Or do you suppose they do not possess sufficient intelligence for such simple analyses? Thus far, they have seldom found observable differences from those they have predicted, regardless of the experiment, even though that experiment is extremely complicated, such as the unparalleled theorization and subsequent construction of the radio proximity fuze, radar, and the Atomic Bomb.

The Earth's atmosphere is constantly bombarded by meteors; can we say, then, that there have been no collisions whatever between small and large meteors? Yet there are many asteroids, and their relative velocities theoretically can approach one hundred miles per second; that is no mean speed, for the greatest velocity of gases in an explosion (non-atomic) seldom exceeds five or ten miles per second. We have still to see any immediately acquire the velocity of infinity, or even any sudden acceleration.

(In justice, however, I must mention that gases expelled from the sun frequently and without warning seem to complete an immediate transition from one velocity to another much greater. Noted scientists are at present investigating possible theories.)

To cause anything to acquire a velocity of light, one must add energy which can still accelerate a mass approaching infinity, always, however, more slowly than the accelerating force which, above all, must not be left behind. Or do you agree with the "orthodox" scientists who stubbornly insist that each atom, each molecule, acts exactly as it would were it as large as the solar system, subject to certain rules, and that the universe could be handled in much the same way with comparable effort?

Will you not, therefore, express yourself a little more clearly the next time you make the statement that an object can be stopped completely by another with but one-millionth its size and one million times its velocity? You see, there are many answers—or, rather, more information must be used before an answer can be given.

If, in such a collision, the objects rebound, their momentum will be added, though the greater velocity will not be exceeded, neither will the other be lessened. (This, of course, is so only if each object is considered relatively stationary and its velocity attributed to the other. Such a consideration is, by no means, unknown to science.) Some velocity, in that case, will be required between five hundred thousand times that of the larger to an infinite number.

If both rebound in a perfectly elastic collision, each leaving with the same difference in velocity as before, a mere relation of one-to-five-hundred-thousand will be necessary; if they rebound with less velocity, they will require more initially; if they do not separate, but continue on together, the minimum initial velocity will be one-to-one-million, and that would be the statement which was made: that, however, cannot happen; there must, in that case, be energy expended in heat, light, penetration, change of shape, compression, and probably many others less well known or even, as yet, undiscovered.

CONSIDER the famous Einstein equation, which is this: the mass of an object in motion is equal to the division of its mass at rest by the square root of the quantity, one minus the quotient of the squares of the velocity of the mass and the velocity of light in a vacuum—$Mv = Mo \div (1 - V^2 / C^2)^{\frac{1}{2}}$. Then the mass of the small object approaches that of the larger as its acceleration decreases upon the approach of its velocity to the limiting velocity of light.

To cause a reaction, one must begin with an action; this action must be in the form of a force; otherwise, any such philosophy is analogous to, but more pointless than, the enigma to the converse of what would happen were an irresistible force to encounter an immovable object; there are scientific laws which govern such encounters, approaching the application of infinite forces to infinite masses and infinitesimal forces to infinitesimal masses; they approach the perfectly elastic encounter, in which the masses and velocities of each are the same before and after the collision, and, on the other hand, the inelastic encounter, in which they are combined to produce one mass with one velocity; this resultant momentum is the same as the sum of the separate momenta before encounter, less that velocity (and perhaps mass) converted into other forms of energy.

Since momentum is equal to the mass of an object multiplied by its velocity, would you mind explaining how it can be possessed by any *thing?* without mass? It is my opinion that you are crudely giving an imperfect idea of that acme of scientific philosophy, the quantum theory, with its wave-mass conception of light.

Weight, Mr. Shaver, is not merely the attraction of the earth; neither has any scientist made that statement for a considerable length of time: you see, weight is the mutual forces of two different bodies (masses) or groups of bodies acting upon a common center, defined as the center of mass or gravity.

Mass, in itself, has never been satisfactorily explained; theoretically, at present, it is used as though it were the static counterpart of energy ($E - MC^2$). Neither is volume now considered to be the space which mass occupies; it is now used as the intervals between the various confines, which in theory also includes time as well as space, under ideal conditions.

Four, you are right, except in one way: you do not go far enough in your explanation. "Orthodox" science is wating with great expectancy for it; they have also tried many times to get a full quart of liquid by combining one pint of water with one of alcohol and they have as frequently failed. Science will accept your statement when you explain sufficiently the conditions under which masses are in their ultimate state, with no space between subatomic particles, with all energy removed, and every other confusing effect dismissed.

—But five, inertia is merely the tendency of mass to retain the same amount of energy that is given it against all interference; this is why such momentum can do work. You are definitely wrong, however, when you state that weight is linked with inertia; no scientist will ever tell anyone that; inertia is the momentum multiplied by one half the velocity and is not concerned in any way with weight, which is the manifestation of a stationary mass acted upon by acceleration, or gravity. An object weighing but an ounce here on earth, like a bullet, can possess the same momentum on the moon, where its weight would be but one-sixth as much; its weight might differ, but its mass, never.

Very light things are easily started, that is true: an object with less mass is more easily affected by the same force, but only until its velocity approaches that of the mass applying the force. As the propelling momentum decreases and the propelled momentum increases, there is less difference until, when their velocities become similar, there is little force which can be applied between them. Regardless of degree of energy, every such object will give back every erg of energy which has been forced upon it.

ARE you sure, Mr. Shaver, that no two masses can occupy the same place at the same time? Why, then, can air be compressed? It is matter. Why can mercury dissolve into gold? How can salts dissolve into water, alcohol, or acid? Everything possesses mass.

While it is true that scientists frequently do not seem to listen much of the time, it is also true that when they speak, one can be sure that they have tried to consider everything and that only in certain instances are there exceptions which they have not mentioned.

How many kinds of waves do you think there are, Mr. Shaver? Science, with all its resources and researches, has been able to discover only two—sonic and electromagnetic. Why do you say that various frequencies of electromagnetic emanations possess different velocities? The velocity of light in a vacuum is one of the few important constants recognized; it will continue to remain so until you, or someone else, can prove by mathematics, physics, chemistry, medicine, photography, or what-have-you to the contrary.

Considering the discrepancy in the radar ranging of the moon, there is also a possible explanation; science has long realized that there are various factors which might interfere slightly with such contact, but not by that much: light has been examined in vacuum and in air; radar has been investigated in air. While light travels slightly faster in a vacuum than radar through air, radar still travels, is nearly as can be determined, as fast as light through the air. (Are you always within one-tenth of one percent of perfect, Mr. Shaver?)

—But am I fighting the wind? If a certain theorem is stated as having been substantiated by scientists, the Army, or some other such organization, it increases the fame of "orthodox" science; ergo, they are lying. —and considered so by newspapers and *Amazing Stories*, of course; everyone believes everything they read in them.

How do we know? Mister Shaver, scientists are not quite fools, regardless of how they have been depicted in the past; do you actually think they have never measured the velocity of light in a vacuum? Do you think they merely agreed together to set up a number which they called Planck's Constant? Do you think they have never measured the force of the sun's radiations upon the moon and other planets? That radiation is exactly in proportion to the amount of spherical surface exposed, though care must be taken to determine the degree of reflection, which increases the force. By their "orthodox" methods they have been able to determine, within a few miles, where those planets will be hundreds of years from now, and thus far there has never been any serious error observed (greater than one one-hundredth of one percent) over a period of several years.

—Oh, yes! I forgot: the planets, according to your theory, are weightless. —Too bad they still have mass.

Too large for such operations, Mr. Shaver? According to scientists, the earth is finer, smaller, less massive, lighter than an electron when compared to the universe.

A back-wall of force? What is that, Mister Shaver? Upon what does its force depend? Velocity? Light? You and I must find *something* on which to agree! This simply cannot be natural!

Foot-pounds is a unit of work; there are many such units, but they are all interchangeable. Nothing ever possesses one of those units unless it is doing work—merely potential or kinetic energy. That energy can be surrendered when the object is permitted to do work, but until then it is as inert as any object within the depths of the earth.

The earth has a relative mass of one; that means that the earth has a unit of momentum which depends completely upon the velocity; others less massive must possess more velocity to attain the same momentum. Scientists may, for convenience, say that a certain force has been applied to a certain mass, but if there is no mass, how can there be action or reaction?

Force is equal to the mass multiplied by the acceleration produced upon it; weight is a force; ergo, a weightless object is one possessing no force. Does that satisfy you? Even though moving with the velocity of light, no mass can exert a force except upon another mass. Then the reaction acts as though the resisting substance possessed no energy whatever, according to relativity, the force entirely relative.

That is the reason scientists must use "x", "y", and "z" as perpendicular axes, placing one mass at the zero point and keeping it there, apply all approaching forces relatively, possessing all the differences of momentum of the encounter. There is no force acting upon any object which is not accelerating in some way; regardless of velocity, its forces are in equilibrium and equal to zero. Any force acting upon it must be oriented to determine the dimensions affected and measured to find the percentage of force which drives it along the "x" axis, that which drives it along the "y" axis, and that which drives it along the "z" axis, each independent of the other, no velocity ever taken away; any future force, acting even in a negative direction, merely adds its own momentum, leaving the former unchanged, but providing, perhaps, the couple which provides a velocity of equal magnitude while the mass is travelling in the opposite direction.

IT IS so foolish to consider that every action has an equal and opposite direction?

Is that why blast waves from explosions exert more force against larger areas? Thus another point for "orthodox" science: if a rocket ship is accelerated by a force acting upon an area, how can any force, unless it be much greater and proportionally stronger, produce the same effect by acting upon a point?

Science musters its resources; from the mountain of knowledge at its disposal comes forth a horde of facts. Some are tossed aside, rejected; others are sorted and filed. Some are ignored; others are passed on for closer attention. Some mean little; others speak volumes; some are useless, but others are omnipotent. A month or two, perhaps three or a year; then science is ready to speak. After a hurried, last-minute discussion and conference, the most brilliant of them steps forward; in halting words he explains: science has searched and found—something; it might be the answer, but it might not; a little more time, perhaps? Three years? No? But science must speak with authority, and to speak with authority, science must know. Facts? There are too few; of thousands of pertinent discoveries, only a few hundreds have definite value. Well, if it is necessary, here is a suggestion; the facts seem to indicate this theory most nearly correct. Science will check again and see; perhaps a little better theory next time, perhaps not.

Blunder? Not they!

Weightless acceleration? Here is the formula: $A=F/M$, in which A is the acceleration, F is the force applied, and M is the mass affected. Let A be equal to G, or gravity; let the acceleration of gravity be equal to absolute zero; then $O=F/M$; when the quotient of a number is zero, the dividend is also necessarily zero; hence, $F=O$.

If that is not sufficient, let M be equal to zero; then the formula becomes $M=F/A$, or $O=F/A$; hence $F=O$.

These are so regardless of the units used, and in them lies no possibility of confusion; the exactness of scientific calculation is easily seen when the equation is examined in all its aspects: let M be equal once more to zero; then $A=F/O$. Since $F=O$ already, then A again is equal to zero.

Blunder, Mister Shaver? To move confusedly or clumsily, to flounder and stumble; to make a serious error or commit a fault, through ignorance, stupidity, overconfidence, or confusion, to utter awkwardly, stupidly, or confusedly—usually with "out". To mismanage, bungle; a gross error or mistake.

Your confusion, Mister Shaver—scientific definitions; your error, use of scientific formulae without the proper units, through ignorance, stupidity, overconfidence, or confusion; take your choice. Your mistake—you are no scientist.—or is that a *mistake?*

Yes, Mister Shaver, do insert the word "orthodox" before proven science; I am quite sure most people will appreciate it, but please do not forget.

I respectfully request that you submit your opinions expressed more clearly in your non-"orthodox" science, if at all possible.

Otherwise, Mister Shaver, any questions?

REPLY TO ROBERT KIDWELL

By *Richard S. Shaver*

MR. KIDWELL, I am going to shock you. I am not replying to the first part of this critique of yours, which is about the Elder tongue, because Palmer is now a better student of that than I myself.

However, the reply to my mundane remarks about inertia must be countered, for you do make me out a fool. I admit the charge, I am a fool. I only insist that the attitude of yourself and science toward the subject makes you both greater fools.

You asked me that in your communication, and I reply frankly, yes I do think they are fools! To tell you the truth, I think there are not a dozen men an earth who think logic that is checkable; that is, carefully analyzed, it will all of it reveal vast discrepancies of sense, so much so as to convince an honest and able and clear seeing mind that this world is really peopled with madmen, and almost exclusively so! Such a mind would have only pity for "science".

Now if you want to go one with the discussion from that basis, perhaps we can agree. I have heard quite common and uneducated men hold forth most brilliantly on that theme, *the world is mad.* Hitler made a good thing of it, too, but the other maniacs stopped him.

First, though, we better cross out science, (as a word) the concept science as generally held is not a usable word in such discussions, it is like saying "the universe says so and so"—or "hot water has an opinion". I admit there are sane scientists, and that they do honest, able work, completely sane, and that the world is infinitely better off for their existence.

But, and it is a *big but,* "science", so-called is not those men. It is a bunch of dunder-heads, over-proud, over educated, bigoted, "sot," holding jobs in "institutions" by means of relatives, political jockeying, tricks and what have you—and giving forth with quite insane pronouncements on this and that. It is not science. It is a myth. This is what all well educated men learn in time, and most of them laugh it off. I can't laugh it off, I'm still disappointed and un-cynical enough to want it different.

These are the men who barred Madame Curie for so long from the French Academy of Science. These are the men who fatten on the work of such people as the Curies, honest, able, understandable work. These are the men, who, when we read them, hide all their meanings in a cloud of formula and verbiage that only a mad "scientist" ever pretends to bother to decipher. And I mean "pretends."

To me, Fort proves this in his books. I have observed something of this sort of goings-on in "institutions" myself.

To disentangle the realities of science from the profound idiocies of "science" is a well-nigh impossible job. I notice you do not manage it very well either.

Since we must battle each other with words which are much abused and blunted weapons, we will have to cross off "science", and substitute a more usable word. What will that word be?

In your second par. where you wave a magic wand, and drop a small object—for instance. You say you have removed gravity. I say you have permitted gravity to act. That is not removal.

You say "scientists have seldom found observable differences from those they have predicted." That is very untrue, and false, and abominable to me. Fort completely proves the mad, base chicanery and hypocrisy of astronomers everywhere in adjusting "found" to predicted. It is not only in astronomy that such chicanery obscures the truths of reality.

This was the case in medieval times, as you would know if you had studied the matter. It is still the case today, except that a more perfect system of open-mouthed acceptance by press and writers and other worthy "lay-men" hides this depravity more thoroughly than in medieval times.

TO anyone who really studies the matter, it becomes very obvious that astronomers do not know the distance to the sun, the moon or the stars with any certainty at all. Yet they profoundly announce the exact orbit of Sirius, the occultation of Uranus by so-and-so, and the predicted position of an as yet unobserved body in space by its influence upon a known body.

Just what is this "science" we are continually referred to? When you find an able man, you find a man engaged in simple understandable experiments, perhaps making a better nylon thread for DuPont, or better frozen foods for Birds-Eye. Outside his commercial application to his subject, he is as lost as you or I.

In some colleges, existing on salaries well known to be inadequate to financing research, we find some able men doing what they can without resource. Along comes a demand for atom bombs, they are drafted, they produce the atom bomb.

Now, where you get involved with scientific formula and bring in Einstein's equation, I say you are getting out of the field on which this discussion must take place. We must use words, and common everyday concepts, to discuss these matters, or be understood by noone but ourselves. We would descend to the scientific level of complete unintelligibility. I refuse to indulge in any such shenanigans. To me, you are disqualified for discussion when I can't understand you. You have to stick to pretty simple concepts and much used words for me to follow. I can't mentally picture a relation of one to one million, and I can't think successfully about it. I suspect noone else can either.

You admit that mass has never been satisfactorily explained. There we agree. I insist that gravity is in the same category, especially out in space, where none of our "scientists" have yet had a laboratory.

You say "science will accept your statement when you explain satisfactorily the conditions under which masses are in their ultimate state with no space between subatomic particles, with all energy removed, and every other confusing effect dismissed."

You are dismissed, Mr. Kidwell, as a confusing effect, right there. If I could do that I would sneer at "science". I do anyway.

You say—"inertia is the momentum multiplied by one half the velocity and is not concerned with weight . . . "

Naturally they take a weight and multiply that by the speed and then have a quantity, which they multiply by one half the time rate of motion. All of which to me, after years of thought about it, brings the conviction that if they knew what they were doing, they wouldn't do it. Especially do I suspect these processes of calling a dozen eggs twelve hen-fruit when you get out in space and find the basic observable fact of it all, the weight, to be reduced to a quantity completely unobservable.

Nevertheless *you* go right ahead and *like* it. I can't agree. They don't know what inertia and weight and velocity and momentum would be, in fact, they only guess. Mine is as good as their's, maybe better, I'm not prejudiced by a lot of other peoples' stored up opinion. I never went to school.

When you tell me inertia is not concerned with weight, all I can think of—"he must be an astronomer."

I say that to get astronomers and scientists together in accord on ony of these problems, and make sense out of the result, is as hard as to get United Nations into agreement and accord on what to do with Russia. Since they can't do it anyway, it's nuts to talk about it.

I say they obscure their futility and inability with a smoke cloud of involved meanings.

I do not know that electro-magnetic frequencies or emanations possess different velocities. I assumed that it was so. I am no scientist. I just don't believe there are very many variant magnetics that travel at the same speed. I have observed a lot of them in action, and assumed they possessed very different natures and consequently different velocities. If it isn't true, I don't care.

TO tell you the truth I do believe they know the velocity of light by a lot of experiment. "Plancks constant" can *be* a constant. I am not agreeing with science nor arguing with it. I am only stating what I think about gravity in space, acceleration of weightless objects, etc. I don't pretend to be right. I only contend my opinion in this instance is as good as the next one's.

From my reading I concluded that light did act up considerably in space, going faster and slower, bending around things and into things. And that astronomy was a science that tried to get along *without* variant light speed, and as a result, didn't know where things were in space, and yet pretended to know. I don't think they can accurately compute the area of the moon's surface, but I know they would *never* admit it. As far as taking their word for it, I refuse! They have been caught too often. Pressure of light on the moon and planets, indeed! Bah.

Yes, I am a schoolboy throwing rocks at teacher. I found out something, and I'm mad about it, a lot of somethings, and I never will get over it. We are a deluded race. We even accept astronomers' pronouncements! They don't know where the planets are, really. (I *read* Fort.)

Maybe light *is* a constant. They *could* be right there, and *still* be awful wrong when they sight along rays of light to determine the distance of a planet, or its position. It curves too easy.

I personally believe light does travel the speed generally given. But I hesitate to say so. "Science" is so insistent upon it, it makes me suspicious!

That they can determine where a planet will be hundreds of years from now, I can even accept. What I *can't* accept is that the planet will *ever* manage to get there at that time!

You will note it's hundred of years away, and we only live seventy. That is like most of the astronomers' profound work, so far away and so long off the deep end, that no one could argue by actual observation.

I never said a planet was weightless. You misrepresent me. They have mass, and they have weight, there is a pull on them from other planets. But I suspect that a slight increase in light pressure from the sun would affect our orbit, these quantities are so small.

I admit I am an ignoramus. I only insist that anyone who accepts all these undeterminable facts like the amount of light to strike the moon as being determined, or the place a planet will be in a hundred years as already figured out—is a credulous ass. I read Fort. I think you should, too. I think we would know a lot more about physics and nature if the "scientists" came down off their high horse, wrapped around with a nice white cloud of mathematical obscurantisms, and told us the truth about things as they really know them to be. But they can't do that, it would unseat too many other officially profound idiots from their "scientific research posts" where they pretend away the days and collect their salaries that a people pays them for honest work. If they told the truth about science, we would have some. But they can't afford to, it upsets too many long accepted applecarts. They can't admit the tremendous errors that have have been foisted upon the public minds so very long.

You are right about science when you say, "the most brilliant of them has stepped forward, in halting words he explains: science has searched and found,—something; it might be the answer, but it might not; a little more time please."

I WAS not speaking of acceleration *of* gravity, since we have no gravity—this is absurd. Your formulas $A = F/m$ etc. may be correct, I won't venture to say. If they are correct, to me they prove that a slight force applied to a weightless mass will produce an infinite acceleration. To you they prove the opposite, apparently.

Why do you say let A be equal to G, or gravity? We have no weight, we do not have a mass. I said the earth formulas wouldn't work in space, apparently you prove it. It is an impossible bit of fancy work to get an acceleration out of nothing pushed by something, they way you do it. Common sense tells us the opposite. But we don't expect sense. It's "science,"

Once, long ago, the word science was synonomous with sense, it meant "checked and verified reasoning." That it does not mean that today you demonstrate very well within this formula and your use of it. I would still like to see it done by a "scientist."

Picking up my Sci. Enc. I look up Kinematics (since it says to after the word acceleration). There I find a dozen formulas for determining acceleration, all of them more complicated than yours, and suspect you of pulling my leg, of over-simplifying, of laying a trap for my dunder-head.

I know there is no arguing with kinematics as the book gives it, it is obviously correct, why didn't you use it? I am not arguing with obviously correct principles of science. but with the assumptions—used as facts.

There is no space here to go into the working out of these formulas, and I say it can't be done correctly because we have never observed weightless bodies.

The basic contention remains untouched, we don't know anything about gravity off of this earth, and its related aspects, inertia and acceleration and mass, are in the same category—out in space. And we don't. Your guess may be as good as mine, but from your words I doubt it.

That anyone has to argue before accepting that a weightless body would be given an infinite acceleration in a non-resisting medium by any largely applied force is to me another sample of earth's general madness. That men in a rocket ship possessing powerful fuel would have difficulty driving a weightless ship at speeds approaching light I do not believe. It is obvious they could go at least as fast as the speed of the gases expelled. (Which you give at five to ten miles a second.) We don't know these speeds in space. We know them only on earth, in air, and in gravity's field. I see these gases continuing to push the ship even when they reach such speeds as light. I suppose "science" would say the gas couldn't leave the jet, since the ship was going so fast it just got left behind without imparting push.

I am not arguing with easily checked and verified facts of science. I am saying that science itself does not do these things, does not exist, does make dunder-headed statements of impossible "truths" about space and stars and moons and suns, and lets them go unchallenged year after year though they are obviously untrue. I say science gets an undeserved amount of worship and blind acceptance that is not good for it, considering there IS very little science that is not either commercial, military or political in its interests. (By political I mean the posts of research given by governments and Funds, or Foundations, where a man must SEEM profoundly correct, and thus cannot go

There *is* disinterested and unselfish research, but not enough of it nor well enough organized to be dignified by the name "science" the way it is generally used. There are many untrue things in text books, that are left there, since there is no organized "science" worthy of the name to remove and correct it.

To throw "science" around as a kind of bogey man which defeats any and all opponents because "science says", is wrong. There is no such science about space, noone knows what is there, nor how objects act in space. Nor how far is a star. They assume these things, and sall them fact. They know it is wrong, but it is completed, no one man can correct the practice.

SCIENCE says Disc ships are spots before fools' eyes. I know they are purposely distorting truth because they are ordered to do so, and that the practice of pulling such wool over our eyes is entirely too general in "science." In such ways "science" is an enemy. It is too easily used against us. The disc ships *DO* exist. I saw the photographs, heard the word of mouth recital of the experience of seeing them, they are a mighty loom upon our horizon and of an alien race—and "science" prefers to keep us in ignorance, uses their divine omni-science to tell us they "do not exist, they are delusions" etc., etc. Such science is the enemy I fight, not obviously correct formulas in books.

You can't check a crooked brain except with such formulas,*they* leave such work alone. Only the honest scientists do such work. The men I hate use fancy phrases to say—"The populace suffers from mental delusions when they see disc ships, it is mass hallucination . . .", etc.

Even those enemy "scientists" call it a mad world, but to a different end. It *is* a mad world.

I do not pretend to *know* more than "science." I do intend to be more honest, more sincere, more open and courageous toward all the secret, duped and dark facets of our life. Where "science" takes an off-the-trail-of-honesty course, for fear of being "wrong", I intend to call them to account. The existence of secret rays, caverns, disc ships and other mighty important secrets is known to "science", yet they take the negative out of that cautious fearful wish to be accepted as right no matter what the cost to the world.

Criminal psychologists, psychiatrists, have stated in the public newsprint that almost all, or the large majority of, criminals have voiced during examination the excuse that they were driven to crime by "a man inside them" by a "voice" by a "ray." Yet "science" is able to brush this almost universal curse of voices off with the phrase "delusions." That is not my idea of science. It is a timid, careful, ignorant, and evil person, hiding a vast and necessary truth because he is afraid of that hidden thing that drove those men he "examined" into crime. Pure funk of the obstacles makes those "scientists" hide these all-important facts from the public. The general sight of disc ships in our skies is another case in point. Do you think all these people had spots before their eyes? They didn't, the scientists know it, yet not a one of them comes out flat-footed and says—"It is obvious that all these observers are not deluded, mistaken people, and that there *is* a menace hiding in our skies and under our seas, in great disc ships."

I am only a writer, not a great scientist, thank God, I can accept the truth where and when I find it without worrying about my scientific reputation to the extent of hiding a world menace from the eyes of the people threatened by it.

I say to Hell with the worship and acceptance of such science. There is no science, when such terrific and everywhere evident truths as disc ships and Elder caverns and mighty ancient ray mech can exist, be used everywhere on innocent people, and "science" still holds forth about "delusions" out of pure fear. I know what the truth is, I have seen it, and I refuse and condemn all such science. It does not exist except as a tool, it has no forthright convictions that it will die to uphold, it has no conscience, no will toward truth. Else it would come out and say the truth loudly and firmly and we could begin to face these parasites and dangers that multiply about us, and fight for what should be ours already but for blind, unworthy, frightened and obeisant "science."

They know, plenty of them, that such impossibilities as I tentatively put forth in my accounts are terribly true of our life—yet for them to say so would be the death of their career. To Hell with a career based on such fear, such bowing before hidden power, such complete lack of spine. To hell with all such science, it is not worthy.

If science has to be that way to be science, we are far better off without it. We

I will quote Fort on astronomers, a paragraph picked at random in three minutes search:

"According to the Lowell calculations, the new planet was at a mean distance of about 45 astronomical units from the sun. But several weeks after April Fools Day, (1930) the object was calculated to be at a mean or very mean distance of 217 units. I do not say that an educated cat or dog could do as well, if not better . . ."

This paragraph, I think, thoroughly answers your statement, which I quote:

"By their 'orthodox' methods they have been able to determine within a few miles where those planets will be hundreds of years from now, and thus far there has never been any serious error greater than one-hundredth of one percent, etc."

The sample picked from Fort of the non-success of a prediction by such an immense error is but one of many, many hundreds he takes from the scientist's own journals and publications. Astronomy as a fake science is seen to be true, when you read this collection of egregious lies perpetrated by the whole body of astronomers. Your acceptance of their ridiculous assertion that they do not err in placing a planet hundreds of years from now is just another sample of the kind of "science" worship which is a great brake on the discovery of truth of any kind. You believed a vast lie when you believed that astronomers could locate anything farther away than Mt. Whitney with any accuracy at all. I wouldn't believe they could locate Mt. Whitney or any other mountain within ten percent of correct with a lens and triangulation. Nor tell you how high it is. You don't believe that?

I quote:

"In the Scientific American, 119-31, a mountain climber says that, in his experience, there is always an error of ten percent in calculating the height of a mountain. (!)

"All that can be said of Mt. Everest, then, is that it is between 26,200 and 31,900 feet high, (before they climbed Everest)."

You don't believe that Scientific American?

Well, the Alpine Journal published a list of eight measurements of Mt. St. Elias, they vary from 12,672 to 19,500 ft. Then D'Abruzzi climbed it, used a barometer, got 18,092 ft.

Now, you think they know where the moon is?

There is not an astronomer in the world who can tell by triangulation the distance of a thing only five miles away. But would they admit it, after all the vainglorious statements they have made? That is not science, that is a madman's world of illusion.

Prof. Newcomb calculates the sun is about 380 times the distance of the moon—as determined by triangulation.

The method of Aristarchus cuts the distance to 20 times the distance of the moon!

Newcomb, in defense against the ancient Greek, says no one can determine when the moon is half-illumined . . . !

Do you think they still know where the moon really is? How far?

Do you think the   radar calculations of the moon's distance weren't doctored so as not to make fools out of astronomers? You are wrong!
need these truths out in the open where we can fight them. Not hidden by slick phrases. No disc ships!

How to picture that spineless acceptance of awful error in astronomy, without ever coming out with the truths they know. How to tell you what the science you bow before, really and truly is to a brave man. Courageous eyes there are in science, yes. But they are directed toward things like Nylon stocking production.

THERE is a mountebank, priest-like side of "science" in the saddle, that is anathema to the clean soul of a man. This is what I deplore, and what every educated man who learns enough to see it cannot stomach, so that he retches every time he hears the word "science."

These mountebanks throttle the patient, honest, courageous work of the true scientists, for it shows them up. These men obscure the truth of such things as disc ships with their profound explanations. They are accepted, and they must not be accepted any more! So were the priests of medieval times accepted by people everywhere, as correct and omniscient. No man can be what they pretend to be is true!

READER'S SECTION

(Continued from page 5)

go to any extreme, or use any and every means within their power to eradicate the annoying (to them) Mr. Shaver?

This could go on forever but I shall withhold the rest of my tirade until I see if Mr. Shaver actually can answer this letter completely and publicly in your magazine, which so far has been prejudiced in his favor. I will admit that if this reaches publication, along wtih sensible reasonable answers I shall owe an apology to Mr. Shaver and his loyal and diligent fans. But before I can even begin to consider the actual existence of Shaver's dero I must have *material proof*. Give me proof and I will give you my most humble apologies for opening my bid mouth. . . . Robert W. Burns, 439 Van Dyke Street, Ridgewood, New Jersey.

Dear Robert Burns:

The caves are easy to get into, hard to get out of. I have yet to meet anyone able and willing to "finance" any safari to anywhere. The biggest contribution we have received is from Dave Fox of Cal. ($55). I mean to return it to him, as we do not have any excuse for accepting funds without repayment. Legally, that is. You have to be a religion, as I get it, to accept money without repayment. We are not a religion.

There is no shred of evidence that I have that you would consider evidence. Just let them rest as hallucinations held by a great many people, and disregard them. The only people I expect to take me seriously are those who have had "phenomena" occur to them or about them. These constitute about one-fourth the population.

I doubted the atom bomb too. I was just as surprised as Hiroshima.

You will never see solid material proof, no one is going to lay it before you personally. This Mystery is not for those who have no reason to believe me. I have said so from the first, but no one listens to the details. They just jump on me for saying what I do to people who do know why I say it.

Space ships have not been seen? Now, Mr. Burns, how about the flying saucers? How about the reef off San Francisco the Navy was looking for? The reef moved off! How about the hundreds and hundreds of reports in the newspapers for a century that could rise from nothing but sight of such ships?

The space ships are antique construction, not built by modern races. Besides they don't come here for washing machines, but for certain other antiques from the caves. I say they do take some of our modern merchandise as well.

They do have trouble keeping their food supply lines intact, they have not only the bewildering complexity of the tiered caverns, they have attacks by savage "dero" to stop their supplies. There are some antique food stocks still intact in imperishable preservation. But they have the best highways on earth, and no weather to interfere with traction. They manage. The caverns do not teem with life, are comparatively deserted. Like the Sahara, they won't support life, but nevertheless you run into it just when you don't want to.

The cavern world is vastly larger than the surface world in area by some eight to twenty times the floor area, and probably even more. This is a point few students of the Mystery get, it is a vast frontier being explored by space pioneers, ignored by us. Our surface world is a flat-land, one plane. Their world is tier on tier, like radio city stacked over radio city stacked over . . .

Surface tunnels, such as mines, are in soft surface rock, subject to water and gas, just as you think. But in deeper rock, pressure makes the rock impervious to water passage, they are bone dry, and for the most part 52 degrees. Some of the deeper levels are too hot to remain in, bearers refuse to go there. Whether this is due to interior heat or local fire pockets deeper in, I don't know. Rock is the perfect insulator, retains both heat and cold. In between are caverns of perfect living temperature. Some very deep levels are filled with ice, seeming to contradict science's dictum of interior heat (of earth as a whole). The caverns are so much vaster than earth's surface there is no comparison, anything can be found there, for even though they have been lived in for centuries, there are still vast areas impassable and untouched, collected gas barriers, cold, rock falls, earthquake slips seal them off. They are the great frontier. Anything can be true of the caves, and usually is. You can send to trading centers for almost anything the mind can imagine, if you have the wherewithal, it will come. There are not only the ancient supplies preserved like the material in Pharaoh's tomb, dry and unrotted for the most part, there are great surface warehouses devoted to cavern supply, secretely to us. . . . Shaver.

Dear Mr. Shaver:

I have collected most of the pertinent parts of the Shaver Mystery as presented in Amazing Stories, including the stories. I have omitted some articles because they held little interest for me directly. Which brings me to my main point in writing.

I imagine the members of the club come from all walks of life but have a common meeting ground in their greater than average curiosity (the serious investigatory type, not the side-line observer type) and bet the average intelligence level is well above the normal of the public.

List members by name, address, and special interest. If their work, profession or the line of their greatest experience or information is different, list that as second. Thus the doctors, the liguists, the mechanics, the artists, the mathematicians, etc. would all be in their respective groups. It is taken for granted that all such will be open minded. They may then readily tackle any development that turns up in their field presented by other members. It is also assumed that members would immediately forward to the club anything they come across out of their own line but of interest to others.

Then when one member has "presented" to him an electrical mechanism about which he knows nothing, he would immediately forward it to the club which would forward copies to members interested and capable of thorough investigation. Some time he might receive just the exact picture or word description of something of interest to him.

Also this division would serve to separate the items from those who "know" it is all metaphysical from the items from those who "know" it is only material and concrete as a highway. Thus forestalling a lot of arguments that serve no purpose. It would also quickly expose any hoaxes. It would also show the club who was actively interested in developments.

The second reason for writing is concerning the Fortean Society. I have read only scattered fragments of Charles Fort's "Lo" and heard several comments on the compilation of occurences he made. It seems that the Fortean Society and the Shaver Mystery Club have a great deal in common in the ground being covered and the problems being tackled. And the hoaxes being exposed. Possibly some members of the Fortean Society are also members of the Shaver Mystery Club. They could be used as a team of correlators to compare what is coming up through Shaver with what Fort discovered.

A possible third reason for writing is in connection with the various mystical and semi-mystical groups and organizations with high sounding names and impressive semantics. I have belonged to some of them at various times and cannot say they are just feather brained. They do have something the average human does not, but it does not have any more important a position in the Shaver Mystery than the activities of the Speleological Society. Just consider their information and claims in their proper classification and there will be little confusion or arguments. After all it is possible that both explanations could be correct. It is the old story of the two sides to every question depending upon which direction you are looking at it.

I imagine that you would get a lot more research done if it were not for the exigencies of living. If the club members were all financially independent they would be investigating everything they could bring up right now. But as with me, making a living comes first as long as one has a family. Also money that must be spent for necessities cannot be spent for investigations of pet interests.

Although I have little at present to add or help to offer, I write to at least let you know my interest remains. As soon as anything concrete comes along my way, I'll send it along. . . . Benamin F. Loudon, 891 W. Masonic Street, Gainesville, Fla.

Dear Mr. Loudon:
I agree with your remarks but I can't seem to add anything. I guess you covered it. . . . Shaver.

Dear Mr. Shaver:

I like the way you perform, Mr. Shaver, and to me your idea explains more otherwise unexplained things than any other I have ever heard of . . . from the oldest legends to our "flying discs". It even simplifies Donnelly's "Ragnarok", without the help of the comet.

And added to all that; I have had enough experience of my own, that like you, I can't prove, to use as evidence. I even have a cave of my own; a dream cave, that I have visited hundreds of times, since I was a small child. Always the same cave, and I'd know it anywhere on earth, if I could ever find it. But I never have.

Mr. Shaver, did you, by any chance, pass through Helbrook, Arizona, in 1928 or 1929, and ask the night marshal for help to protect you from them? I am the man who was marshal, and if it wasn't you, then there is someone else who looks a lot like your picture running loose around in the country, and from the same thing, apparently. You have said that you spent some time trying to escape from the rays and the voices. So, also, was this man. And believe me, he was in one awful jam.

I have Charles Fort's books, and I have been a member of Tiffany Thayer's Fortean Society for three or four years. I have been up here in this frozen, unresponsive North country for six years, and up to date I haven't found one single person who will, or can talk about such things. So it leaves me a little on the lonely side.

Mr. Shaver, did you ever see a Hopi Indian Snake Dance? I lived for fifteen years on the other side of the tracks from them, and I have never heard of them making a mistake in their methods of rain making. Evidently they have access, some way, to weather control machinery that just never fails. An Apache Indian told me once that he saw his mother "pray" a hailstorm AROUND her corn patch.

I had a "guest" in my jail who told me he saw a Navajo medicine man with a "magic stone" with a round opening in it that, looked through as a telescope, caused a . . . well, as he described it, a twisting or bending of space and motion, or something, that produced vertigo and maybe unconsciousness if carried too far.

And with a straightjacket and a padded cell staring me in the face . . . I will have to admit that I think I believe all this. Quien sabe manana, y porque?

Keep up the good work, Shaver; there are maybe a few of us who are not completely blind and deaf to all the things right under our feet. . . . Lee Summers, Route 5, Box 87, Grantsburg, Wisc.

Dear, Dear Lee Summers:

There are an awful lot of us who aren't blind and deaf, but we've got a battle on our hands if we expect to tell anyone.

About praying hail around, I used to get my cabbage watered when I set it out by just asking for it. It would rain right down the row and then chase me into the barn—and dry as dust everywhere else. There's weather machines setting down there they can do most anything with. Did you ever see the weather charts after a big hurricane? Some of them sweep right up to New York, then suddenly change their mind and curve around and up the coast.

Glad to meet a Fortean. One of my greatest pleasures is reading Fort's chapters on astronomers. Greatest humor on earth. That's humor, brother.

I think there are quite a few Indians still extant in the caves, which is the secret of the Indian's rain making.

Used to have a recurrent dream when I was a kid. Floated down through successive floors of strange deserted, somtimes peopled buildings. On and on. Then I learned a little girl did it to please me. I still have floating dreams, same reason. There are some swell people down there, lucky for us. And the real devils. Heredity or environment? With a devil its heredity. . . . Shaver.

Dear Mr. Shaver:

I have been following your stories with interest and with a certain amount of anticipation. I am interested in what you write about and hope that it will really lead to an enlightening period of knowledge and civilization.

Now I'm of an inquiring mind and I would like to tell you a story that is true in every detail but unreliable because it comes from an ex-convict, therefore unbelievable. Will you read this and tell me what you think?

Like the most of the men who have their freedom taken from them I spent many hours wondering what it was like on the outside of my prison walls and wondering if there was not some way of getting out sooner than the officials would release me. And time hung heavy on my mind.

Hours on hours would go by with only thinking to relieve me of the boredom brought on by the inactivity of confinement. My only enjoyment lay in the private and secret process of my mind as I built fantastic situations where I could adventure in. And like a good many other prisoners who have so much time to think, I became a Philosopher. Not just a home-run Philosopher, nor one who knew all the various theories of life from the books other had written.

Books failed to satisfy me on the reasons of life. Things seemed so hopeless and useless, especially from my point of view. I was slated to serve a term of 5 years to life, and what the hell was the point of living if I were only to be released after I was an old man and ready to die anyway. With this point of view, I was actually on the point of ending it all. The coward's way out? I don't think so, now when one was as full of life as I was and young. The confinement to me was slow death. And deather for a dog at that. To die under those conditions would be a great adventure. And eventually one must die anyway, so why wait until the dogs of a corrupt prison guard system could have their way with me.

With this thought in mind I would lay on my cot night after night and wish I were dead. Yes, I even challenged God to prove he was God by doing away with me if he was so great. Now here is where the unbelievable happened. I noticed each night various new sensations swept over me. I seemed to be in a sort of jumbled, sensous, and elated condition, expecting and knowing something was going to happen. I wanted to die and my request was about to be fulfilled. My joy knew no bounds. At last I would make the Grand Escape and something told me I wouldn't be dead either. That is, dead as the world would think.

Suddenly one night while lying on the cot I seemed to shift as though I were two persons, and there was a separation taking place. With this shifting sensation I felt as though I were floating about three feet over the cot instead of being in the cot where I knew I was laying. My eyes were closed, but I was never more awake in all my life as I was at that moment. My mind was in a whirl trying to analyze what was happening to me. All at once I sensed someone near me and heard them say "shall we slit his throat". Needless to say this frightened me. If anyone was going to cut my throat, I wanted to see who did it. I tried to open my eyes and found them sealed to my efforts. I tried to move and could not. I became alarmed at the position I found myself in and suddenly felt myself dropping back to the bed, where I reunited with the body I felt I had left there. The minute I got control of my body I opened my eyes and jerked my arm up. I saw nothing. But I certainly felt someone stroke my cheek very plainly. And all fear left me at once.

Many times I have been asleep since then and thought I was dreaming but just before waking I seemed to be coming back from being some place while my body slept ,and I would see my body lying on the bed just before I woke up. The conviction of my mind traveling independently of my body would be strongly upon me.

Now what do you think of this? Say I'm crazy and we'll just both forget it. After all I know.

Dear X:

I know what you mean about inside looking out. Also had a friend who woke up floating. He thought it was his body levitated, though. I dream of floating a lot, quite often.

Such sensations can be conveyed with the telaug ray. They can also come from other sources. You're not crazy. They are very common phenomena, in occurrence. But they mean a lot more than anyone realizes.

Whether the Star Rover type of soul travel is a true thing or not, lots of people think so. I don't know. I think it's done with mental impressions, for no particular purpose but amusement. I could be wrong. I think this enforced solitude and privation and lack of distraction or diversion in prison results in peculiar opportunity for development of the inner mental powers. For me it resulted in a thorough going over of my whole thought processes and checking out the fallacious and unworthy. That's philosophy, though it's an abused word. You and I have much in common, as a result of having had such discipline, such time to think. In common with other thinkers, we had time to think. Maybe it was a loss. Probably not. Some achieve thinking, some inherit thinking, some have it thrust upon them. I say thanks. . . . Shaver.

Dear Mr. Shaver:

A word about the Club Magazine—two sharp brickbats included with a bouquet. Mandark (first issue) is a terrific disappointment. Pages sixteen and eighteen made me wish for a hot soapy bath, gargle, and mouth wash. Is it necessary, Mr. Shaver, to be quite so darn vulgar as page eighteen??? That page is torn out (the top three-fourths) of my magazine and burned, and strips of plain paper pasted over three fourths of page sixteen. Also the front cover is blanked out. PHEW! I will enclose ten cents in stamps (in case the next issue has a like naseous cover) to pay for sealing the envelope containing my second magazine. Aside from above comments, the contents was very interesting. I am looking forward to the next copy. . . . Eva Mead Firestone, Upton, Wyo.

Dear Eva Mead Firestone:

Well I guess the truth is vulgar, that's the way it happened. On the top of eighteen I'm only telling the truth about what goes on in a man's mind. And the same with the thunder receptacle, the only way you could get such a picture is by unobserved accident—they would spoil a film, but did not see the unmentionable fluid until it was dried in the dark, and the print or negative—it looked positive enough—was irrevocably formed. It was such an accident that proved the reality of what lies behind dreams, just as I tell it to you. I am not making that up, if it's vulgar, then life is vulgar. It is true that many chemicals are sensitive to light, and change as in a film when light strikes. That cover was not nauseous, it was very fine. Eva, you worry too much! You can hear and see worse things than that in every bar, tavern and most of the restaurants in town—especially if you look inside the minds there, most especially so. . . . Shaver.

Dear Mr. Shaver:

To begin this letter, I must admit that much of Shaver's ideas are rather vague to me. This is not intended as a slur upon the man's works; but rather an excuse (or apology, whichever you will have) for my own difficulty in reading between the lines.

You have undoubtedly heard of many people who hear voices. A large number occupy our asylums. I'll just hope and pray that I don't join them. Well, to get to the point, I suffer under the same illusion (?) and at times the results are rather startling. It doesn't occur often, but enough to cause a bit of wonderment.

While speaking to an acquaintance the other night I mentioned these little episodes and at his suggestion began keeping a little book handy in which to take notes in case it happened again.

To cut this whole thing short, the following is what I took down. "you know the atom better than anyone. What is this job they're going to do?"

There is it. Off my chest and onto yours. What you can do with it, I don't know. If you can apply it to the mystery then I'll feel that I have been of some use. If not, well, at least you have read rather odd little story and perhaps found it amusing. . . . D. Bruce Berry, 359 Haight Street, San Francisco, Calif.

Dear Bruce:

I don't know the atom better than anyone. I hope I don't know what they are going to do with it. If I do know what I think I know, they are going to blast themselves off the earth and most of the rest of us with them. What's left probably won't matter, the earth will be too full of radiation for it to get anywhere. I do not find the prospect amusing. It is odd!

Odd that men can't keep from killing themselves.

About one out of four hear voices, won't admit it. I suspect the rest won't admit it, and hear them too. Ergo everyone hears voices, only a few will admit it openly, a lot indirectly, two thirds deny it wholly. I don't believe them. They are unobservant, attribute what they hear to sounds and forget about it. . . . Shaver.

Dear Mr. Shaver:

I will attempt to give you an outline of at least part of my experience at Bendix during and following the time I operated a spot welder. I did not know of the Shaver Stories while at Bendix. In fact, Shaver had not started to write at that time.

Shaver states he operated a rotary spot·welder. That the transformers for same were located on the floor above, that each arm of the welder had a separate transformer, that only one transformer produced any effect on him.

I gather that the welding machine was one of the old type using A. C. current? This is important. What kind of condensers were used in this line? How long did he operate the machine before the first effcets were felt?

The direct current type of spot welder which I operated did not come into use in this country until very shortly before we entered the war, about 1938 or 1939 and there were only a few in use then.

The inventors of the D.C. welder were a company in France and just before France collapsed the company moved to the U.S. By the end of the war there were several thousand of these machines in use.

Shaver states he could understand what people (who were near the line while the welder was operating) were thinking about.

Did their thoughts just pop into his mind, similar to his own thoughts but recognizable as of foreign origin or did he seem to "hear" their thoughts or was the effort a sort of picture mental image?

When he was done working and left the plant what effects were most noticeable on the street or trolley car? Have the effects or the extra sensory perception work off completely at this date or are they permanent? Were you at all naturally sensitive before you started to weld? Did you notice this and that when you were away from the plant among or near any group of people that without saying anything or doing anything other than just walk along or sit in a trolley that almost invariably one or two people out of say every 10 or 12 would suddenly become very conscious of your presence? (I have jumped right into the heart of one of these angles right now).

I would like very much to have a personal answer from you on the above question and an especially detailed one on the last one.

I will try to give you a brief summary of my own experiences on the welder. After I had operated the Seacky welder (DC) about a year, in August 1943, I began to notice that when I was near any power line, house wiring, or walking under overhead lines that there was a feeling of a wave of force flowing from the line through my body. This was in no sense an electrical shock as is generally understood but might best be compared to the force of fine streams of water under terrific pressure. The effect was more annoying as the weeks went by.

I also began to notice a similar but not quite so rotating effect while near telephone lines. There seemed to be a cloud like effect clinging around telephone and cables especially. I could even feel the force wave effect from the overhead cables while riding past them on the trolley cars. I soon began to notice I could feel the motor of the trolley car and could feel force currents being drawn toward the trolley motors from any part of the car. To say I became slightly worried would be putting it mildly.

In the plant near the machine, force currents or waves began to be felt from many adjoining machines. The welder (because of its large copper electrode) seemed to draw most of the force currents toward it. Thus far I had not noticed any effect attributable to human origin.

One morning in September about a month after the effects started, the air-raid blinds had been opened and for once it was broad daylight in the shop. I was working on a routine job when one of the young engineers from another department came in with a small rush job he wanted welded at once. He had the print and proceeded to show me exactly what he wanted. We were both bending over the bench in front of the welder when I happened to look directly at his face. It seemed to suddenly become covered by a semi-transparent film or cloud. His features faded and in their place appeared the features of another person—different eyes, different colored hair. I stood and looked at him for about 20 seconds. He or whatever it was, stood and looked at me without moving. Then the strange face seemed to fade away and at the same time recede into the true face of the young man underneath. The dissipation of the imposed face lasted or took about 5 seconds before it was completely gone and I was standing there weak, my mouth open and staring at the young man who had come in with the rush order. The young man did not seem to be conscious of the elapsed time when I had observed all this but went right on talking about the job as if nothing had happened.

This is hard to take but I assure you it was still harder for me. No one can realize what a jolt you could get from seeing anything like this until they have experienced it themselves. It was several days before I had myself convinced that maybe after all what I had seen was real and that I was not suffering from illusions and the beginning of insanity. Days passed before I saw this particular phenomena again. The next time was later at night at the guard house near the front gate, on the way to work. I had purchased some small items and on arriving at the plant I went around to the guard house with my slip to retrieve my package. There was only one guard on duty in the house. I handed him the check and he began to look for the package taking his time. I waited a minute and then happened to look directly at him again. His face began to change again the face of another person was imposed. You could see through the imposed face for a few seconds and then it became the only one visible (solidified is the word) and again about 20 seconds duration. Again 5 seconds for dissipation and the guard started to move normally again, found my package and gravely handed it to me and I walked out without a word being said.

After a while I began to see that some of the operators of the lathes and milling machines near by were watching me a little more than was necessary. This was now about three months before I left.

Some of the wave force effects flowing toward the machine became stronger and more annoying. Right back of me as I stood facing the welder were two engraving machines. I noticed that one of these machines was in operation an especially strong force wave was felt. The operator was a little fellow about 35. I noticed when I turned around he was usually watching me and not his machine. The strong force effect from his machine continued to increase in strength and severity intermittently. A pipe ran down from the ceiling to his machine to carry the electric waves to the engraving motor; about two feet above the machine was a box switch inserted in the pipe. The particular phase or current originating from the engraver began to become, at times, too strong for me to take. I thought I would have to get away from the welder and stay away, but it was intermittent. I turned around just as the engraver sat back down at his machine. The wave increased with unbearable strength. Then I had an inspiration. On the switch box of the pipe hung the large roll of masking tape the engraver used. I walked over to the engraving machine, lifted the roll of tape off the pipe and laid it on a nearby work bench. The oppressive force wave was gone. I gave the engraver a very dirty look and he looked back with no expression at all. In ten minutes the force wave started again. I turned around and the roll of masking tape was back on the box switch I went over and laid it back on the bench again. This performance was repeated at least 10 times that night. The last time I took the roll and put it in my own tool box. I was so angry and upset I just wanted the engraver to ask me for it. He never did.

I did not notice any extremely bad force wave effects when other people were operating that particular engraving machine although they all had the same habit of hanging their masking tape on the pipe switch box. The main point I want to make here was the fact that no one would say anything either about what I did or the effects of the machine. Even to the end. Any mention was taboo with the group leader, foreman, or head of the department.

So a very serious situation developed. I began to feel both angry and resentful but at the same time the increasingly strong effects were so startling that I decided to hold my resent in check and learn as much as I could while I could.

I had the right general idea of the cause of the effects and although I was not at all certain as to how strong or how bad they could get I determined to hang on as long as possible. The welder began to work poorly and for the next two months there was constant trouble and breakdowns.

Whenever the machine broke down, instead of hunting up something else to do I would wander around the plant simply watching the machines and feel the current and wave effects that I now began to find everywhere. I saw the guards do something in the main assembly room that to this day I have no explanation for. I was standing in one of the doors of the assembly room which was very huge. About a block long and half block wide. It was filled with rows of assembly benches each row a doublt one. There were probably four or five hundred people working on the lines, most of them women.

There was a sudden tense feeling in the room. Someone called loudly for the guards. At lease 4 or 5 guards came on the double. This was on the other side of the room from where I was standing. There was a huddle of guards and one or two women. Then the guards fanned out and one of them went down each side walking fast. When the guard on my side passed me I could see that he was holding one hand out toward the benches and he had two half dollars in his hand loosely held. As he walked he was klinking them together. This made no impression on me until the guard who had gone around the room the other way passed. He too had two half dollars in his hand and was holding it out toward the benches. The guards were within six inches of me so there is no mistake about what they had in their hands or what they were doing. They were not looking for something but were feeling for something. They paid no attention to me whatever. I stood there for a minute or two longer, then I heard the maintenance man testing the welder across the hall so I went back.

What were the guards feeling for and how could they find anything by feeling. I am quite sure none of them ever operated a welding machine.

This will give you an idea of my experience. There is a lot more. Most of it is made up of little things, but some were not so little. A few are hard to take or unbelievable. At least 2 or 3 might have some bearing on the Shaver Mystery.

Pseudo heart attacks were experienced. They were recognized for what they are. Pseudo heart attacks are just another angle that really needs to be looked into. There is no doubt if a person who was badly run down or an aged person was forced to experience one of these attacks it could and would prove fatal. I am afraid that you won't have much material for your magazine here as most any of it would be bound to antagonize somebody, as a moments reflection will show you. I can and will furnish you with the rest if you wish.

If you could supply me with the answer to the questions in the first part of the letter it would be appreciated.

Just one more thing. What Blood Type are you? The writer is type O.

I have a theory that people of different blood types are affected in different ways by the welding machines. I have a few fragments that I have managed to worm out of other former welders. Most of them have been so badly scared by their experiences that they shut up like a clam. They are afraid of being considered insane.

Where I differ with you in part is of course obvious. I assure you that you may be right in a good many ways though. . . . William Fitzgerald, 800 W. 32nd St., Baltimore, Md.

Dear Mr. Fitzgerald:

Your letter is interesting to me, very. About the welder, I worked on three different machines, two of them stationary. I am not sure the rotary was the one really responsible, but to my observation it seemed so. That was in '32 in the old Ford Plant, run by Briggs body in Highland Park. I have no doubt of this type of current producing such effects over long exposure. I also had telepathic phenomena at the stationary machines, so it was not any peculiarity of the machine, but the strong intermittent exposure, I suspect. The rotary happened to be better in sensitivity, and I wanted the story to sound as true as it was.

I can't say for sure it was AC. As I recall it was direct, but I don't know. According to your data it must have been AC; I suppose you are right. My skill was limited to changing the points and hitting the spot.

I don't think it matters; it is the flux of the high frequency fields formed by the intermittent solenoids crashing through the body continually, stripping the nerve insulation. I have also had peculiar stories of these effects from welders, electric as well as spot. They clam up when you ask questions.

My first sensitivity was my greatest; I could hear three floors of men thinking all at once. After I heard the cavern ray, they cut my nerves, and I have steadily decreased in sensitivity since from frequent ray-cuts. Now I never hear thought, except over a strong ray from caves.

I have noticed such scenes as you mention with the guards and the half dollars. This is common, but the police will not admit it. They are searching for the source of ray deviltry which is complained about to them. They think it is in the machines themselves just as you did. Naturally they never find anything. But they get bamboozled by ray tamper and voices into thinking they are always going to locate the trouble. They go through such performances mainly to quiet the fears of the complaining victim, people like yourself who suffer such phenomenon as the strange face on a friend. But they never open up about it, probably through fear of panic effects.

The strange face projection you noticed is a particular kind of projection machine. I have seen it used to decorate the whole landscape for a picnic. Each tree had around it a gigantic face, human and beautiful! It is a multi-projection device for such decorative effects.

I could hear the thought afar, like voices, but different. It is hard to picture. Got no images, just words and abstract meanings. This is speaking of direct telepathy from people around. It may have been due to ray work, too, remember, as was some of your experiences.

On trolley car, it was most noticeable. Your words tell me you suffered from tamper, this indication of certain people around you as being responsible and being aware of your telephatic hearing is a regular tamper, it results in rash actions, and gets you in trouble, which the dero delight in doing.

Your experiences with the masking tape and workers around you is of this type. It results in attributing your hearing to others around you, the detrimental rays to machines near you, and finally results in your being put in an insane asylum. This, (they say) is a racket they get money from. The government pays $1.50 a day for keep of inmates, it costs around thirty-forty cents. Somebody pockets the difference. Actually I doubt they get it, but they may delve that deeply into our politics.

I think we have both been caused to be naturally telepathic by the welders, and then the ray people, seeing our awareness, started to cause strange phenomena for pure deviltry. Give a kid a bee-bee gun. I don't know my blood type. . . . Shaver.

Dear Mr. Shaver:

I wouldn't miss the Shaver Mystery Magazine for the world. Mandark is the most interesting thing I have ever read.

Some things have happened in my life that tally with the "Mystery". In this letter I would like to relate them in detail for what they are worth to the solving of the mystery.

December 26, 1925, my wife and I were about to leave her father's house where we were spending the holidays to make the midnight train for Yakima, Washington to get our belongings and ship them to Othello, Washington, as I had obtained work there.

It was snowing hard with a foot or more on the ground. We stepped out onto the porch and my wife said, "I forgot to get a handkerchief." As I stood waiting for her to come out again I heard a voice say, "It will be a fair day and I will give you a safe trip." Just that, not more. I went into the house, told my wife what I had heard spoken to me and told her we would take the old Dodge touring car and drive to Yakima in the morning. We set the alarm for six o'clock and went back to bed.

It was still snowing when we left town about seven thirty the next morning. We had about 20 miles of deserted road to travel before we got to the ferry across the Columbia River at White Bluffs and to our surprise several cars had been ahead of us and the snow was well broken.

At the ferry it quit snowing and soon the sun was shining. We did have a safe trip with sunshine most of the time. But here is the surprising thing. Just as we got out of the car in front of the house it started snowing again and snowed all night and part of the next day. Does this not offer some proof that your weather machines are a reality?

In June this year while driving to the bus stop to pick up my daughter I suddenly heard sweet music playing the "Great Speckled Bird".

I have tried everything I can think of to make it happen again but have completely failed.

Also in June of this year I had to repair the water pump on my car. It has four 2½" bolts and two 3" bolts holding it to the motor block. One of the 3" bolts was broken a little below the head and I screwed the broken stud out of the block with a small stilson wrench. I laid all the bolts together on the work bench and went ahead repairing the pump.

The pump repaired I looked in a scrap bolt box for a bolt to replace the broken one. I found one that would do but it had a square head instead of hexagon. Back at the bench I started putting the bolts in the pump housing and there were six whole bolts instead of five I expected. I thought I must have taken a bolt out of something I shouldn't have, so I took one of the 3" bolts and went to the motor, but could not find any place it could have been taken out of. It was a 3" bolt exactly like the other 3" bolt, same rust, same corrosion, same wrench marks on the head, believe me. I looked them over good because by this time I knew something extraordinary had happened. I have that extra bolt here in the house, and a reliable witness that was present when this happened and was just as mystified as I. If I could find someone who was working on a Hupmobile water pump at that same time and if they were minus one of those 3" bolts that would prove something.

The thing I can't understand is why do the cavern people play around like that.

Pardon me if I tell one more incident before closing.

While setting here in the house reading one evening at about 9:00 o'clock I had an irresistable impulse to hurry outside, which impulse I obeyed. As I opened the screen door I looked at the sky about 150 feet above the horizon. I saw a streak of fire across the sky from east to west on a perfectly horizontal course, from as far east as I could see until it disappeared to the west. I judge the time of passing to be about 5 seconds. It must have been several miles distant and traveling at tremendous speed. It could not have been a meteor because it did not veer toward the earth. I cannot help but wonder why I had that impulse at just the time this space ship (?) crossed the horizon.

Does the Shaver Mystery explain these phenomena? That is what we want to prove. So far I am on the Shaver side. Maybe you are wrong but you will have to prove it to me.

I am a seeker of truth and I believe I can recognize it when it is presented to me. I have scrapped a lot of my pre-conceived theories since reading the Shaver Mystery.

Fan letters should give the club a clue as to where the most populated caverns are located. I suggest that a large map be obtained and a gross or so of pins. As you read the fan mail where mysterious phenomenas occur stick a pin in the map. Where the most pins accumulate is where the cavern people are most active with their mech. This may lead eventually to the discovery of openings to the caverns.

Well I guess I have had my say and I hope you are not bored with this letter. I want to do all I can to help solve this mystery. I am with you all the way. . . . Frank D. Matchett, 2702 Melbourne Street, Houston, Texas.

Dear Mr. Matchett:

The cavern people often do play around. There are pranksters even among the Tee groups, and kids often get at certain of the ray mech and raise a lot of surface mischief. My files are full of such incidents . . . letters, newspaper clippings, and the like. Such things go on all the time, and are evidence of the life under our feet. If the public could be made to understand the cause of thes phenomena, they would cease to be so puzzling and mysterious. Your ideas about the map, I like. We will try it when we have more letters to work from. . . . Shaver.

Dear Mr. Shaver :

During the war I worked at Rhor Aircraft, as a spot weld operator on a graveyard shift. I took the midnite shift mostly because I have insomnia from 3 A.M. to 6 A.M.

I had not been working more than 6 months when I began to feel someone watching me and later began to see smoky, hazy forms take shape above the machines. These shapes seemed to be talking in a humming voice. They surrounded me at odd times. At home my husband began to see them standing over me and later seemed to be aware of someone standing behind him too! After a few months of this he began to hear machines operating while he was lying in bed and it became so pronounced he quit his job in aircraft only to find the noise increased and then was added to the din "voices" arguing back and forth.

We changed bedrooms and shifted beds. We then decided it was something coming in through all the electricity generated in the large Electronic spotweld machines. So I too quit the spotweld operating and took up metalsmithing. Two weeks later a smoke haze form came to me and actually kissed me on the cheek. Then, since then we have not been visited by the forms and gradually the arguing voices have ceased—thank goodness.

We both are ardent fans ever since you gave us a logical explanation of the phenomena we both experienced—Rhio Myers, Hilltop Village, Chula Vista, Calif.

Dear Rhio Myers:

Sure am glad to meet people who have had same type of phenomena as I. This is the biggest and most important fact of our modern civilization, yet is as old as witchcraft. The kiss you mention was a good sign, given to reassure you that your troubles were being attended to. They are simple long-range projection phenomena, yet they are beyond modern science to reproduce, because the ancient rays were so conductive of nerve impulse energy. Any thought picture can be projected life size, so almost any kind of form or phantasm may be seen.

I too quit spot welding, and fled around the country, finally to Newfoundland, where I found even more profuse phenomena. But there was good ray in Newfoundland too, and it turnel out ok.

Arguing voices: these are the tero trying to get the deros to lay off you. (I would guess.) Actually dero and tero are only ancient words I use—the cavern people call dero "rods". Tero are just "friends." They do a lot of work for us, and they get no payment.

If they had not interfered, the "rods" would have put you in the hospital, as they are strangely persistent in following and persecuting people they fasten on. You had a narrow escape.

Stick with the mystery, I am sure people like yourself will really get a lot of valuable info on this most interesting hidden side of our life. The flying saucers are something to think about. . . . Shaver.

Dear Mr. Shaver:

I hope I am not too late to receive the first two issues of your new magazine, for it would be a shame to miss anything on the Shaver Mystery, especially after reading every issue of Amazing Stories and Fantastic Adventures. I have been a fan for more than five years now, and I certainly do not want to miss the novel "Mandark", which title alone has a strange but true meaning in itself.

I don't want you to think that I am trying to hoax you or gain the limelight as some people have already tried to do, but since you and Mr. Palmer have asked for anything that would pertain to the Shaver Mystery and to do our own investigating, I will give you some of what I have learned since the Shaver Mystery began in January of 1945.

First I searched the public library for anything that I could find and took notes on anything that I thought would be useful. What I found you know yourself, and most has been mentioned in Amazing Stories. One book by Col. James Churchwood states that certain rays if properly filtered can produce a growth, neutralize it, or retard it, also that these rays can cure cancer, T.B., etc.

I have some ideas of my own on how to filter out these rays and intend to build my own equipment and experiment along the line mentioned by Churchwood.

Next, Spiritualism has been mentioned in Amazing Stories in which Mr. Palmer, you have formed their own opinion and I am more convinced to believe as they do. Spiritualism is not a hoax, what I mean is these people believe just what they claim and are very sincere about it. Those mediums do not throw their voices or have loudspeakers and projectors secretly installed. I don't think that they have ever heard of a dero, and if they have there are very few of them that do know. The majority believe that they are their departed loved ones that speak to them. My experiences with Spiritualism began about four months ago. I have been to two sources. The voices that came to me seemed so real and natural that I could not tell whether or not it was a clever impersonation or the real party. The doctor had a clear sounding voice and spoke good english. The Indian guide and others were not so clear at times. Their words were sort of clipped and the letter C was T, e.g. curl—turl or curly—turly. Another thing a party whom I have known for several years and is related to me by marriage had been under treatment by one of their healers. This healer told her to get X-Ray tests for T.B., which she did. Now the strange part about it is that the hospital staff could not locate the X-Ray photos when her doctor wanted them and they haven't been found as yet. At the seance the doctor told her that he had destroyed the X-Ray photos because he had been mistaken when he told the healer that she had T.B. I myself don't quite accept his answer for destroying the X-Ray photos.

Their healers can cure for I have seen it done. My wife had gall stones and our doctor said that she would have to go to the hospital. She was pretty sick at the time. My Father-in-law mentioned this healer. I was skeptical but he said it would do no harm to try it, so I consented and after two treatments my wife began to pass the gall stones. She weighed about 85 pounds at the time and now she weighs about 135. He cured a girl friend of my sister-in-law of cancer of the breast. Another woman that had been deaf. A man who had worked in the shop with me was shot in the eye with a B.B. Gun when a child and has never been able to see with it since, went to him. Now he can see again although not as good as with his other eye, but he can see. Call it what you will. I cannot understand it. I have seen it done and whatever it is, it surely hasn't done any harm.

That is how I got into Spiritualism. I wanted to find out just what they are, spirits or dero. I do not think they are spirits but I cannot judge for sure.

There is one more incident that happened which I would like to mention. This happened about 1943 or 44 just outside of Clarkston, Mich., which I read in the Detroit Times. The people involved was an in-law to my mother-in-law's first cousin. I never knew the full details of the accident till just last February when I visited with this cousin who lives just outside Pontiac, Michigan. These people were killed by fire or explosion that occurred in their basement home. So the police and fire departments claimed. But this is the story I got from my mother-in-law's cousin.

About four or five days had gone by and he had not heard from them. So he and his wife went over to their place (her parents). The door was locked and had to be forced open. They found her mother (who weighed nearly 300 lbs.) had been thrown against a partition knocking part of it down and a dresser which pinned her husband underneath it and the baby which he had in his arms. The bodies were all burned to a crisp. The man's eyes were pulled completely from their sockets. The gas stove was not on and the heating stove was not lit. There was paper, wood, and coal in the stove. The table was partly set. There was a five pound sack of sugar on the table. The table cloth and sugar sack were burnt completely but the table did not have a burned mark on it. The glass in the china closet was melted right out of the frame, but the frame was not burned anywhere. The police and fire inspectors claimed that the heating stove had gas in it and exploded. But this does not explain how a woman that weights nearly 300 lbs. could be thrown against a wall with such force. If the concussion from an explosion was strong enough to do this it would also have taken the door off the stove and broken the windows. It does not explain why four bodies were burned beyond recognition. The table cloth or glass pane, while nothing else was destroyed.

I understand that this property is for sale but hasn't been sold as yet, and that no one lives there as yet. It seems as if they were trying to get away from something when the accident happened. I wondered what frightened them, or had they found something?

I myself would like to go see this place and I might when I get the chance. I don't like to ask the cousin any questions or mention his name. He may not like it and I don't know him any to well, but if I get the chance I am going to find out more from him. . . . Charles A. Marcoux, 1714 Arizona Avenue, Flint 6, Michigan.

Dear Mr. Marcoux:

Please stick with your intention to work on growth rays. They are exd, what is left when sun-fire gets through with matter. I have a lot of data from other experimenters along this line that is accumulating. Sooner or later we will get it to you to help you.

About spiritualism, I am interested just as you are. I do not disbelieve in spirit but to my thinking they could not live on earth in so tenuous a form. I think they may have been something of the kind in the far past when conditions were different. But I could be wrong about it all, although I know ray people fake spiritualist phenomena. There may be also true phenomena, though it would be hard for us to separate the true from the false.

I do think that one in the ether of space there may be a kind of spirit life.

About the fire you mention, I see no way to find out now if it was or was not a murder by ray, and no good would come of learning that now. We are after those angles that will result in good for men from the resulting publicity—like the discovery of how the Elder race made beneficial rays, stim rays, penetrative rays andother advanced mech. Proving the Mystery will result in more intelligent application to the problem of getting this info into the hands of modern surface science. That is why we wan to prove it. . . . Shaver.

Dear Mr. Shaver:

I found the first two issues of the Shaver Mystery Magazine highly entertaining and very thought provoking. The same can be said for the Mystery in its entirety.

Due to my being in the service, I had not kept up on the latest in the scientifiction world and did not become aware of the Shaver Mystery until about a year ago, but all my life I have been very much aware of a "farce" existing and to a great extent influencing some of our lives.

For example, I had been a grocer for eleven years prior to my induction and expected to go back to being a grocer as that was all I knew and I was always able to make enough money in that line to satisfy me. One night, out in the Arizona desert, I had a dream in which I saw myself operating a large red inter-urban type trolley car. I told my buddies about it the next day and we all laughed and forgot about it. Two weeks later I was discharged due to a shoulder injury incurred before my induction. So back home I went. Due to the wartime restrictions and the rationing the grocery business didn't look too good to me so I cast about for other employment and finally wound up as you have already guessed operating a trolley car. But not a big red one, just the ordinary type seen everywhere. I was dissatisfied and wanted to quit and the company transferred me to Washington River where those big red cars run from Washington to Pittsburgh. So here I am, just as I saw myself in that dream and I might add that the dream never recurred to me until after I had been here for some time.

That is only one of the various dreams I have had which have reached fulfillment. Whether you have found the answer or not I am not at this stage prepared to say but I will say it is possible.

You might mention to your readers that copies of the Club Magazine are in the class of collectors items and as time goes on will increase in value. So care should be taken to preserve them in good condition. I suggest a book cover made from cellophane, held in place with scotch tape on the back of the cover and the inside of the back. Sheet cellophane can be purchased at any variety store, 3 large sheets for ten cents.

By all means keep putting out covers on our magazine along the lines you are now using. I do think the second cover is a little under standard set by the first one. I am not complaining as I think we are getting a big fifty cents worth. . . . Dean B. Weltmer, 70 E. Chesnut St., Washington, Pa.

Dear Mr. Weltmer:

Can't tell you anything about that red trolley car, except that I have heard from cavern people the tale that they have heard of robots the Elder race built which could fortell the future. It is just one of those things we have to take or leave. I can't figure myself how anything could see into the future. As to my way of thinking it is always now, and time is a man-made illusion of regular change. But maybe they could look into the next now. Or perhaps it is an extra sense you were born with, in which case I would cultivate those dreams.

Thanks for understanding how much it really costs to put out a magazine. We are racking our brains for a cheaper method. Until then you'll just have to accept quality instead of a lot of pages and filler. When we get the cheaper method, we are going to put out a larger magazine, filled with data and letters from readers. It is a beautiful little magazine, and we are going to try to make it more so if we can. We are definitely going to complete the Mandark novel in the present size so that it can be bound. . . . Shaver.